Dedalus Europe 1

General Editor: Mik

CW00350056

Infinite Possibilities

Translated from the French
by Liz Nash

Infinite Possibilities
(Immensités)

Sylvie Germain

Dedalus

Funded by
THE
ARTS
COUNCIL
OF ENGLAND

Dedalus would like to thank the French Ministry of Culture in Paris and The Arts Council of England in London for their assistance in producing this translation.

Published in the UK by Dedalus Ltd, Langford Lodge, St Judith's Lane, Sawtry, Cambs, PE17 5XE

ISBN 1 873982 23 2

Distributed in the United States by Subterranean Company, P.O. Box 160, 265 South Fifth Street, Monroe, Oregon 97456

Distributed in Australia & New Zealand by Peribo Pty Ltd, 58 Beaumont Road, Mount Kuring-gai, N.S.W. 2080

Distributed in Canada by Marginal Distribution, Unit 102, 277 George Street North, Peterborough, Ontario, KJ9 3G9

First published by Dedalus in 1998
First published in France in 1994

Immensités © 1993 Editions Gallimard
Translation of Infinite Possibilities copyright © Liz Nash 1998

Typeset by RefineCatch Ltd, Bungay, Suffolk
Printed in Finland by Wsoy

The translator would like to thank the following: Kate Love and Matthew Avery for their help and advice, and the British Centre for Literary Translation at the University of East Anglia for providing a bursary funded by the European Commission.

THE AUTHOR

Sylvie Germain was born in Châteauroux in Central France, in 1954. She read philosophy at the Sorbonne, being awarded a doctorate. From 1987 until the summer of 1993 she taught philosophy at the French School in Prague. She now lives in Paris. Sylvie Germain is the author of nine novels, a study of the painter Vermeer and a religious meditation. Her work has so far been translated into seventeen languages.

Sylvie Germain's first novel *Le Livre des nuits* (*The Book of Nights*) was published in France to great acclaim in 1985. It has won five French literary prizes as well as the TLS Scott Moncrieff Translation Prize in England. The novel ends with the birth of Night of Amber and his story is continued in *Nuit d'ambre* (Night of Amber) in 1987. Her third novel *Jours de colère* (*Days of Anger*) won the Prix Femina in 1989. It was followed by *L'Enfant Méduse* (*The Medusa Child*) in 1991 and *La pleurante des rues de Prague* (1992), published by Dedalus under the title of *The Weeping Woman on the Streets of Prague*.

THE TRANSLATOR

Liz Nash was born in Northern Ireland in 1952. She was educated at Bristol University where she obtained a first class honours degree in French and German.

Until recently she was Assistant Head of Modern Languages at Winchester College, where she taught for fifteen years. She is now a freelance translator.

Her translations include Sylvie Germain's *The Medusa Child*, and she is currently working on a number of projects including *Fou d'Echecs* by Rezvani.

'A heart that can be satisfied within the limits of place and time knows nothing at all of its own infinite possibilities.'

ANGELUS SILESIUS

'Let us go and seek what is ours, however long the journey.'

F. HÖLDERLIN

CONTENTS

THE FLOWER
OF PASSING TIME

1

Prokop Poupa was a pariah. He had once been a teacher of literature, but had been obliged to change his job. Every door in the world of education, from university to nursery school, had been closed to him. What had opened instead, on two occasions, were the doors of prison.

For years now he had earned his living as a cleaner. He washed the corridors, windows and stairs of a whole block of apartment buildings in an outlying area of the city, and was responsible for sweeping up the dead leaves in autumn and clearing the snow in winter from the pavements round about.

As time went by he had more or less come to terms with his fall from grace. He accepted the consequences of the choices he had made with dogged stoicism, and wasn't prepared to compromise in any way just in order to make things easier for himself. They had taken away his job and his passport, and in return had given him a broom, bucket and floorcloth. Prokop Poupa was a prisoner on probation within the borders of his own country, and all he could do now was get on with sweeping one little patch of it.

The staying power he had always demonstrated in politics had not, however, been quite so evident in the matrimonial sphere. He had been through two divorces, and none of his other relationships had stood the test of time either.

Before ending in divorce, each of his marriages had produced a child. By his first wife Magda he had a daughter, Olinka, and by his second, Marie, a little boy called Olbram. Olinka lived out in the provinces now, so he hardly ever saw her. As for his son, he only had custody of him for two evenings a week and an occasional weekend.

What with his failures in love, his erratic contact with his children, and the fact that he had no more than a handful of friends left – since most of those he had known in his youth had emigrated to the West – Prokop Poupa was a rather isolated figure, struggling to get by on the ever-shrinking margins of society to which fate had consigned him. Because of this it was really essential for him to concentrate all his attention on the very few pleasures that were still available to him, and to learn to appreciate any aspects of his unenviable lot, however trifling, which had even the slightest degree of charm or beauty, or offered a few moments of unexpected respite. He became an expert in the art of discerning subtle nuances, and this saved him from being eaten away, like so many others in his situation, by bitterness and despondency.

And that was why everything about his apartment, even the lavatory, was so important to him. His many years of wielding the broom and floorcloth had developed in him a spirit, not of meanness or servility, but of mockery, and of a modesty that was slightly tinged with madness.

2

Prokop Poupa's home was his castle. It consisted of a bedroom and a fairly spacious kitchen. The bedroom overlooked a busy street full of noisy cars and trams, but the kitchen faced on to the quiet courtyard side, so Prokop had separated a small corner of it off with a wood and glass partition, thus creating a cubby-hole for his bed where he could sleep in peace.

The courtyard was a huge rectangle enclosed between a group of five- or six-storey apartment buildings, and planted with trees. In the summer months it was filled with a muddled tangle of branches; silver birches grew there, along with beech, apple, lilac and ash trees, one tall linden tree, and a great luxuriant undergrowth of bushes, ferns and wild grasses, with a few dark red roses poking through to the surface.

Adjoining one of the apartment blocks was a building about two storeys high which jutted out into the courtyard. In summer it was half buried by plants and bushes. It had grey roughcast walls and a flat zinc roof with a little raised square of glass in the middle, and looked like an artisans' workshop or a warehouse. In fact it was nothing of the kind. This peculiar building hidden away amidst the undergrowth was an Evangelical church which resounded throughout the year – every day at vespers, morning and evening on Sundays – with the voices of the faithful lustily singing the psalms and proclaiming the splendour of the Almighty.

In spring these solemnly joyful voices added a counterpoint to the frenetic babble of mating birds and shouting children; in summer their soft tones vied with the frenetic rhythms of pop music blaring out through wide-open windows from radios and various sound systems; in autumn they harmonised with the monotonous pounding of the endless rain; and finally in winter they grew a little hoarse between walls that were saturated with cold and darkness.

Thus life went by in the grassy, woody courtyard hemmed in by dingy, roughcast ochre or yellow-brown walls, and sanctified by the presence of a warehouse dedicated to the Lord.

From his fifth floor vantage point, Prokop could look down over the whole courtyard-garden. That gave him a sense of freedom and deep peace, which was reinforced by the fact that when he chose to gaze upward, beyond the roofs bristling with gables, turrets, chimney stacks and aerials shaped like rakes or roosts, he could also see a great expanse of sky. And so he was happy living up there, perched among the clouds and foliage like a jackdaw nesting in a high cliff hollow.

There was nothing bird-like about the people who lived around him, however; if anything, they were more like wild animals.

The upstairs neighbour, Mr Slavík, was a rough-hewn giant with an enormous square head, no neck, and shoulders like a fairground wrestler's. He always looked fierce, angry and rather wild-eyed, but that might have been because Prokop only ever met him on the stairs, when he was invariably struggling back up to his flat, red-faced and snorting from the effort of carrying a heavy load. Sometimes this was a bag full of beer bottles, but more often it was his old dog, which he took for a walk twice a day despite the fact that its

15

hindquarters were paralysed. The walk consisted of no more than a few steps around the block. The crippled animal would move forward very slowly on his front paws only, while his master held his belly up with a wide crimson wool scarf, the ends of which he used like puppet strings to steer him along. It was a pitiful sight, but it was also quite ridiculous. If ever children or passers-by were tempted to mock, however, Mr Slavík nipped their laughter right in the bud by rolling his eyes at them in a furious, threatening manner.

As for the old animal, he seemed to feel nothing but an infinite weariness. People could laugh at him as much as they liked; he was deaf, and his protruding eyes were filmed over with cataracts. Certain well-meaning souls in his building had ventured to advise Mr Slavík to have the poor creature put to sleep. His response was a deafening roar, after which they didn't broach the subject again.

The people downstairs were called Slunecko. They spent their time having rows, during which Mrs Slunecko shouted a great deal in a boozy voice which was also remarkably loud. The noise was bad enough then, but it rose to an even higher peak when there was football on television. She sat glued to the screen through every single match, uttering piercing cries of frenzied joy or fury which poured forth in a torrent of cheerfully obscene profanity. During the last World Cup she had bellowed so hard that by the end of the fifth match she had lost her voice and from then until the final had had to be content with making sinister rattling noises. Because of her, Prokop always knew when an important match was due to be broadcast, and on those evenings he went out to a café.

Even so, Prokop preferred the fishwife Slunecko to his neighbours across the landing, the Zlatopírkos, who, beneath their stiff and starchy, respectable façade, were in fact dangerous two-faced bastards. When they passed Prokop on the stairs they pretended not to see him, as if they had suddenly been struck blind, or Prokop's sixteen stone had melted into thin air. But they did give him nasty, tight-lipped, sidelong glances, and kept a close eye on everyone who paid him the briefest of visits. It didn't worry Prokop; the few people who made the effort to come up and visit him were all on file and labelled already, and, like him, had been relegated to the dusty waiting-room of History.

3

To say that Prokop Poupa gave a great deal of attention to everything in his apartment, even the toilet, is not to imply that he was the least bit interested in decorating his home: far from it. This was attention of quite a different order.

His kitchen was a shambles; there were books sitting among the saucepans, and piles of banned pamphlets alongside tins of food, pot-plants and empty bottles. The mess was even worse in the room on the street side, which was where the children slept when they visited. Two stowaway beds were buried somewhere under a jumble of boxes and pieces of furniture filled to overflowing with clothes, toys, files and books.

When he was small, Olbram had scrawled graffiti on the walls in felt-pen and pencil. Then, when he was about eight, he discovered the fabulous story of Robinson Crusoe, and embarked on the ambitious project of painting a fresco to the glory of his hero on one of the walls. But his fresco was transformed by a turn in events when a friend of his father's, Radomír Kukla, was sentenced to eighteen months in prison. At that point Olbram decided that, instead of surrounding Robinson with an entire exotic jungle complete with wildlife as he had intended, he would limit his work to the castaway's beard alone. Every week he put a new brush stroke under Robinson's chin, thus adding seven centimetres to the length of his beard. His fresco became the calendar of Radomír Kukla's imprisonment. When Radomír finally came out of prison, Robinson had a beard five hundred and forty-seven centimetres long which wound around the room in sweeping arabesques. The beard had become a jungle in its own right, not least because Olinka, on her visits to her father, had contributed to the fresco by decorating the huge luxuriant growth with details symbolising seasons, feast days and birthdays. Here and there one could see, hanging from the little curls, a sprig of lily-of-the-valley or a rose, an apple, some stars, an Easter bell, an April fool fish, a candle, some snowflakes, a branch covered in russet and gold leaves, a moon, some mushrooms or a cherub with a cheeky smile. The very last picture on the beard was of a brightly-coloured bird.

And then there was the toilet. It was a long, narrow recess, with one little window high up on the far wall which looked out on to another wall less than a metre away, and therefore let in only a meagre amount of daylight. Despite the limited amount of space in the room Prokop had built shelves along the whole length of each wall which were crammed with empty jars, spare light bulbs, nails, candles, pieces of string, old rags, worn-out shoes and various tools. Just in front of the toilet seat hung an ancient, blue-green woollen blanket, suspended by curtain rings from an iron rail right up close to the ceiling. It was faded, dotted with holes and frugally patched, and when it was pulled over it enabled the person sitting there to feel completely cut off from the world. Prokop was obsessed with creating partitions.

He had also placed crates on either side of the seat to act as shelves for a few books, the toilet roll, an ashtray, his lighter and his packet of cigarettes. The chain had a little extension cord for Olbram to use. And Olbram, being an artist of some versatility, had decorated this string by attaching a little copper bell to it. This meant that when he pulled the chain, the roar of the flushing water was accompanied by a bright, graceful, tinkling sound.

Another striking feature, up at the join between the ceiling and the wall with the little window, was a patch of damp which Prokop described as a living sculpture. It grew in fits and starts; there were long periods when it almost seemed to have disappeared, then suddenly it would burst forth into a new phase of burgeoning growth. At that point the yellowed paint would blister and crack, and take on subtle tinges of green and pale ochre. This plaster waterlily had been created at some time in the past by a leak from the pipes of Mr Slavik's toilet, and by now it was spreading over on to the adjacent wall.

Far from regarding it as a matter for concern, Prokop took great pleasure in watching it grow. There isn't usually time to watch things actually living. For all things and all matter have a life of their own, however slow-moving and unobtrusive. Olbram thought they should stick tadpoles on to the ceiling, in the hope that they would grow into frogs. As far as he was concerned, a waterlily without a frog or a toad living in it was an error of taste.

It was thanks to the hours he had spent dreamily contemplating this lotus of the lavatory that Prokop won his finest claim to fame: as the Lord of the Household Gods.

4

That happened not long after Radomír Kukla was let out of prison. He, Prokop and a few others met at the Little White Bear, their favourite tavern, which was situated in an alleyway near the river.

During one of the many digressions in which their discussion became entangled, Radomír talked about the legend of the household gods, and proclaimed that it was essential for everyone to give shelter in their home to a guardian spirit. When you live in a place where walls have ears, or even weasel's eyes, any protection, however unorthodox, is worth having.

The question arose as to where the gods should have their shrine. Radomír declared straight away that his would go in the kitchen. That was his favourite room, not so much because he loved food as because of certain lessons he had learned through bitter experience.

Radomír had once made documentaries for television, but he had been hounded out of the media and now earned his living as a window-cleaner, when he wasn't rotting in prison.

He could no longer use his reporting to provide his fellow-citizens with a clearer view of the world, so he washed their windows instead. The job didn't offer much consolation, however, since rain and city pollution ensured that the windows were filthy again almost as soon as he had cleaned them. As for the work he did behind the scenes to fight against the implacable, petty-minded régime in power, it never seemed to get anywhere. In fact, far from changing things, his dissident activities had done nothing to date except embroil him in all sorts of problems, anxieties and unhappiness. His love life was similarly strewn with failures.

And so he turned to cooking, the only activity that gave him the satisfaction he was denied everywhere else: that of seeing his labours come to fruition.

Since coming out of prison Radomír had experimented endlessly with recipes for cakes and pastries. He was forever kneading dough, measuring out ingredients, weighing, mixing, sprinkling, adding toppings and fillings, feeling, sniffing, tasting . . . It gave him a whole range of things to do that stimulated the senses and kept his mind fully occupied, thus releasing him for a while from brooding on his worries and disappointments. Best of all, he was able to produce a concrete, rapid, result that couldn't possibly get him thrown in prison, was of no interest to the censors, wouldn't be sabotaged, and tasted good as well. No other activity, for nearly two decades, had brought him such pure and complete contentment.

Every time he went to his oven and took out an apricot and almond tart, a cheesecake, a cinnamon or rum gâteau, a plum brandy roulade or a liqueur soufflé, or bit into a walnut candied in honey or an orange-peel fondant frosted with brown sugar, he experienced a pleasure that went far beyond his nose and taste-buds and spread into his whole being. He felt as if he were biting into the very stuff of life, and tasting a little of its beauty and goodness. It was the same sense of delight and achievement that a child gets from standing back to admire his own magnificent sandcastle.

And that was why, on that evening when he was talking with his friends in the Little White Bear, Radomír declared that the proper place for the god's shrine in a home was the kitchen. There and only there, he said, should the benevolent guardian spirit of a household be located. And he raised his glass in a toast to his household god with the white chef's hat.

The first to reject Radomír's cult of the oven was Radka Nebeská. She had recently spent a few months washing dishes in a canteen – one of many little jobs she had done since being thrown out of university – and as a result had come to loathe the kitchen sink and everything associated with it. As far as she was concerned it was simply not possible for the presiding spirit of the home to be enthroned in a room where there was greasy, gurgling washing-up water. She then ran through the other possible rooms in an apartment, and after some hesitation plumped for the attic, since that was the part of her own flat where she spent most of her free time. She and some friends had set up a makeshift printing-press there, and although the machines were pretty archaic and materials were scarce, she worked away in it like a beaver.

When there was a shortage of paper or binding-canvas Radka scoured the entire city, even if it meant going right out into the sticks. In the end she always tracked down what she wanted – a few reams of copy paper, some glue, or a little bit of canvas that might have been intended for an awning or even a funeral canopy – and then back she went with her booty to her attic workshop.

Radomír's suggestion was also rejected by Jonás Tupík, a small, exceedingly thin photographer who never seemed to eat anything. He proposed the bathroom. That was where he developed his photos, he said, and for him there was no nobler place in his apartment. Beyond that, however, he made no attempt to justify his choice, even though he could easily have set his bathroom up as a place of holy purification. Lengthy discussions were not much to his taste; he was sparing in all things and unobtrusive almost to the point of total self-effacement.

For Aloïs Pípal, an actor who was banned from the stage, the obvious choice was the dining-room. He had a passion for model railways, and had built an enormous track in his home. He had even bored a hole in the wall so that he could watch the trains running through a tunnel from the dining-room into the hallway. This was a compromise solution; he would have tunnelled into the bedroom had his wife not forbidden him to do so. The only god Aloïs could conceive of within his four walls was one in a miniature stationmaster's cap.

Barbara Bambasová, known to all as Big Baba in homage to her ample figure, chose that rather cramped, peripheral area, the balcony. The important thing for her was that the shrine should be outdoors, because she loved birds and could do wonderful imitations of their songs, as she now proceeded to demonstrate by giving a remarkable impromptu recital. Her repertoire ranged from the crystalline trill of a blue tit to the gracious chirping and twittering of a warbler, with the drumming of rain on tiles and the gentle howling of the wind along the gutters thrown in for good measure. It was clear that the only household god Big Baba could contemplate was a feathered one that would nest under the eaves and flit round her windows scattering silvery notes.

Viktor Turek went to the other extreme and shoved his guardian spirit down into the cellar. He played the jazz saxophone, and the basement was the one place where he could blow away to his heart's content at top volume, not just in his own apartment block but, because he was also a heating engineer, in other basements as well. And so he gave his household god fiery colours: the reddish glow of the boiler room and the golden gleam of copper among heaps of black coal, with the dull roar of the fire and the strident rasping of his saxophone for added effect. In fact he left all that to the others' imagination, since he himself made no contribution to the discussion. Viktor was the most taciturn of men.

Then came Prokop's turn. By now the choice was so limited that all the others were expecting Prokop to put his household god in the bedroom or the living-room. In fact he did neither. To everyone's astonishment, he chose the toilet.

There was something rather shocking about this decision to relegate a guardian spirit to the privy, and his friends were quick to tell him so. Prokop paid no attention and stuck to his choice. He began his plea in defence of the lavatory by referring to the wonderful work of primitive art that was growing on the ceiling of his own toilet. Once he had explained that it was a living sculpture, he proceeded to give a detailed description of the damp, puffy plaster flower with its ever-multiplying petals.

'It's not a flower,' said Big Baba, 'it's just a pile of grot, and one of these days it'll come crashing down on your head!'

'No, no, you're wrong,' he said, seized by a sudden thought. 'It's the flower of passing time.'

5

And then, swept away on this surge of inspiration, he embarked on a lengthy eulogy of the lavatory. Anyone would have thought that his plaster flower had grown a great number of little roots and rhizomes which had surreptitiously crept into his brain and were now suddenly sprouting forth in the form of garrulous words. It wasn't surprising really; after all the hours he had spent daydreaming under the flower of passing time, an idea was bound to germinate in him sooner or later. Now, stimulated by the greenhouse atmosphere of a smoky bar-room that stank of beer and fried food, it was finally bursting into full bloom.

'The lavatory,' he declared, 'is the one place in the home one cannot avoid going to. It is actually possible never to go down to the cellar or up to the attic. Some people never go near the balcony, or don't have one at all. You can leave a study completely unused, and let dust pile up on the living-room furniture. You can wash in a bowl or even not wash at all – too much dirt won't kill you, whereas an obstruction of the bowels or bladder will, as Ticho Brahé discovered to his cost. You can cook on a portable stove and eat in a corner of your bedroom, or conversely you can sleep on a bench in the kitchen if you're short of space. If need be you can reverse the roles of all the rooms in your home. But the toilet is different, it has a particular purpose for which you can't use any other room. Not unless you want to let your life go to rack and ruin. It's not for nothing that when we're in prison they just shove a bucket in the middle of the cell. It's the perfect way to inflict yet more humiliation on us.

'And this is a room that every member of the family, one by one from the little kid to the grandad, has to go into several times a day. We're talking here about a place that is indispensable, irreplaceable, and what is more entirely democratic.

'But that's not the real crux of the matter. What makes this haven of democracy truly special is that, rather like Descartes' wood stove, it is quite definitely a holy place of meditation. As soon as you place your posterior on the toilet bowl, you are inescapably confronted by the human condition in all its crudeness, and you really are forced to admit to yourself that the Emperor has no clothes. Yes indeed, the Emperor and Empress are also just two among many omnivorous, smelly, dung-producing mammals. Try and think yourself superior to your fellow creatures when you know that. The toilet is an excellent school of humility; it's difficult to mistake yourself for a god in there. It sets the record straight.

'So far so good, but that's only the beginning. Remember when Descartes came to the realisation that both our senses and our rational judgments could be unreliable? Having made that sad observation he didn't stop there, but got going again straight away on mercilessly tracking down false ideas. And so the epic history of doubt was set in motion. It's the same in the toilet. In there the Emperor has no clothes, which means that he can get a sense of how small he really is. His crown falls off his head, so all of a sudden his brain feels lighter and he can think more freely. And then his spirit can begin to converse with the beast, which after all is very much what the Emperor is when his trousers are down. And that's why the toilet has a far greater purifying power than the bathroom, where you only wash the surface of your skin. In the toilet it's your inside

24

that gets purified. Your whole being is flushed out and your brain is purged.

'And of course as soon as you have purification, asceticism comes into the picture. You start with the stove where the philosopher sits cogitating and then move on to the confessional of the repentant sinner. You've got to probe the limits of your own wretchedness if you're to have some chance of genuinely healing your soul, because then you're digging right to the depths of the infinite divine. You have to delve very far down into yourself, into your own guts, to find a means of access to the Almighty. You know how it is in our own lives, when we're thrown on the scrap-heap and everything is turned topsy-turvy? Well, that's nothing compared to when it happens in the world of the spirit. The prophets were already proclaiming it in the Psalms:

' "From the bottom of the pit I cry out to you, Lord!"

'It's always from the bottom of a pit that people cry out most loudly to God. What about Job? There he sat on his dung heap, shrivelled, scrofulous and flea-ridden, and yet he still ended up better off in the eyes of God than his handsome, smart, right-thinking friends. The same point is made in the Gospels, and then St Paul reinforces it. So does St Thomas Aquinas when he states that our bodies are the concrete expression of our souls, and that everything our bodies are subjected to has profound repercussions on our souls. Thoughts like these, which can seem quite sublime when they're dreamt up in a monk's cell or a library, take on a very different character when you're shut up in the loo thinking about them on your own. In there they are firmly rooted in solid flesh and putrid matter. They don't skip over the problem of our fleshly nature; they accept it warts and all, in all its inconstancy and baseness.

'In short, the lavatory combines all the qualities that holy places of meditation have – in fact it's even better than they are. It is *the* place to go if you want to experience the finiteness of your own humanity and get a glimpse of an infinity that's beyond rational conception. So it's the perfect spot for a household god's shrine. And if you won't accept my arguments it's because you're a bunch of boorish half-wits.'

'When it comes to half-wittedness you're way ahead of the rest of us,' Radka replied calmly.

And Radomír merely added: 'Listening to you singing the praises of solitary confinement and mortification makes me think that maybe what you need is another little spell in clink, or even in a mental asylum.'

By now the others were dozing off, and Big Baba was actually fast asleep in front of her glass; at this late hour, her snores resembled not so much the fluty pipings of an oriole as the muffled, booming quack of a Canada goose.

Even so they decided that before getting up from the table they must settle the matter of the location of the shrine once and for all, and under the influence of beer, wine and fatigue, they agreed to grant the title of Lord of the Lares to Prokop. Not that they were really convinced by his arguments, but he had intoxicated them with his eloquence.

6

And so Prokop found himself honoured, just for an evening, with the title of Lord of the Lares, in the same way as jesters used to be disguised as kings at carnival time, just for a day. But as then, the mockery on this occasion had a very serious side. Prokop's meanderings were not just theoretical, they were based on long years of experience.

For throughout his life Prokop had indeed made use of his lavatory as a solitary retreat and private reading room. By now he had passed on the habit to Olbram, who went there to devour comics and his favourite books.

But Prokop didn't just read in there; more often than not he broke off from his book and started daydreaming. These lapses in concentration were not unconnected with what he was reading at the time, in fact it was usually something in the text itself that sparked them off. Phrases, or sometimes just words, suddenly and unexpectedly leapt out of the page and took on a strange resonance and a disquieting density. There were even times when, for a fleeting moment, a word assumed a tangible form which was faintly visible, and seemed to flutter for a few seconds just above the open page, like a frail transparent insect. It was at those moments that Prokop let his attention wander from the flow of the text so that he could concentrate on this one little scrap of language that had just detached itself from the page and flown upwards into the shrill silence. It could be a rare word, or a perfectly ordinary one. The sudden beauty of a line of poetry, the expressive force of an image or a phrase, the surprise created by an unusual positioning or inversion of words, a felicitous metaphor or concisely expressed idea: any of these was enough to make him stop in his tracks, pause for a moment, then go on the lookout for some hitherto undreamt-of meaning or some deep, hidden enchantment that might emerge from the expression. Then his thoughts would begin to roam at leisure over the terrain of language, things and images, and rather than seizing on a precise idea, he would start to spin an endless web of daydreams.

After these mental detours, Prokop didn't abandon the books he had been reading. On the contrary, he returned to them with greater vigour and insight than before. He sank back into them as if into a shady, fragrant undergrowth. He dreamed on the inside of words, in the texture and savour of their flesh whose hidden folds and recesses murmured with echoes, assonances and breaths. And whenever he felt one of these dreams welling up inside him with particular intensity, he would instinctively pull over the faded blue wool curtain so that he could feel more alone in the depths of his rêverie, and concentrate his imagination.

And then, in the bluish semi-darkness which enveloped him as he sat enthroned on his toilet seat, bare from his waist down to his calves, with his book gaping open on his knee, he saw himself as a grotesque king who had received the gift of noble dreams, a half-wit whose brow was suddenly bathed in a light of wisdom. And always at such moments he felt how close he was to real life. It was as if the mystery of life was just about to reveal itself to him fully, palpably, luminously. Sometimes this feeling was so acute that it almost made Prokop feel dizzy, like a tightrope walker teetering unsteadily on a steel wire stretched above a double abyss of wonder and terror.

But he was never able to find the right words to describe his feelings and intuitions, and even though the door to the mystery of things stood half-open, he couldn't get across the threshold; and so his exalted mood would abruptly collapse and topple into gloom, and suddenly he would feel that his backside was bruised from having spent too long sitting on the toilet seat. By the time he stood up and pulled up his trousers there was a red ring on his buttocks, his lower back and calves were frozen, and his mind was completely exhausted.

He was not discouraged by these repeated failures, however, and went back every day for another reading session, not in the expectation of any precise result or blinding revelation, but through force of habit and for the pleasure of dreaming.

One day he was leafing through the latest issue of a literary review with pages as fine as cigarette paper and printed in very faint mauve, when a short poem caught his eye. It was a translation of a few lines from the vast epic poem *Kalevala*. Some lines from the introduction to the first canto were quoted in an article on the great epic poems.

'Words turn to water in my mouth, / squalls in the throat, a rain of speech, / they rush in torrents on to my tongue, / they drizzle against my teeth.

'Little brother, my young brother of gold, / fine companion of my youth! / Keep me company in the song / come and join me in the game of the runes (. . .)'

It was a shock, a physical sensation; the dense beauty of the lines took on material form and texture the very moment he read them. Each word became a speck of rain or sun or wind, or a flower: the sort that grows on rock plants, lichen or ivy. And the vegetable, mineral, granular words filled his mouth and melted in his throat.

It was a sudden, luminous, icy downpour, a gay drumming of silvery drops of rain, a dance, a joyful sensation on the tongue.

'Little brother, my young brother of gold, fine companion of my youth (. . .)'

Out of these words friendship burst forth with the vigour and force of a sparkling spring gushing out of a rock. All the sharp sweetness of brotherhood was there, plain to see.

And best of all: 'Come and join me in the game of the runes (. . .)'

Come and join me in the game of the runes, in the beautiful song that enchants and bewitches: at the feast of words gleaming with rain, blood and mud, bathed in glistening light; at the circle dance of words as rough as tree bark and rock, as silky and soft as fruit; in the hunt for words that run on the moor, haunt the forests, swim in the sea, shine beneath the ice and fly across the sky in banks of steel-coloured clouds and flocks of wild birds with raucous cries that sing in the trees; at the marriage of words with the whole space of heaven and earth.

Runes: incantations carved in stone and wood, words hollowed out in raw matter. Roars rising up from the bowels of the earth, from the depths of rivers and silver birch forests, from great, metal-glinting oceans and huge milky skies; from open sea, arid lands and purple heaths, from snowy wastes and icebound waters. Echoes of cries from the eager, red-glowing throats of beasts and the harsh, dark throats of primitive men. Roars at once muffled and magnified by the raucous song of the wizard bards. Voices of the earth at its beginnings when a race of men rose up like a horde of trees marching against the wind in the full blast of a storm. A splendour of sounds from the depths of the ages.

And now that ancient time was here, sitting almost tangibly in Prokop's hands. It lent colour to the flower of passing time that bloomed above his head, blew in the wool of the blue curtain with its galaxy of holes, shed a dazzling brightness into the half-light of the place, and created an infinite space between the walls. It filled the toilet flush with torrents of icy water, a heavy white swell and squally gusts of wind. And the little bell that Olbram had hung at the end of the cord was a meteor.

Sitting on his toilet seat, Prokop was a bard dazzled by the unfolding of an age-old dream. The world was being born around him in a rustle of mist, runes and silence.

Prokop sat on for a long time like this, completely absorbed in a prodigious daydream of earth and words, until suddenly there was an uproar which brought the game of the runes to an end.

The din sprang not from the depths of the ages and the distant shores of the Baltic, but from the Sluneckos' apartment where a quarrel had just broken out. Doors were slammed, chairs overturned, insults hurled in torrents. They were runes of a kind, shouted out by the shrewish Mrs Slunecko in the only way she knew.

THE GIFT OF THE MOON

1

Prokop daydreamed like this all the time; shut away in his toilet behind the blue curtain, with the cracked flower of passing time above his head, he wandered deliciously through mazes of words, listened attentively to the rustles and whispers of silence, and pondered patiently over dreamlike images. All these hours of rêverie left behind a residue of wisdom which gradually built up in him like a silty deposit. It was a humble wisdom, steeped in gentle madness.

And it produced the kind of fertile soil in which just about anything might start to grow.

But time kept passing and nothing happened. The plaster flower turned bumpy and yellow, and more and more blisters grew on it, puffed up with emptiness and damp. Day after day went by, punctuated by Prokop's broomstrokes up and down his allotted patch. It was a time of dust and gloom, enlivened only occasionally by reading, evenings at the Little White Bear, and visits from Olbram and Olinka.

A rich soil on its own is not enough; it also needs to be dug, turned over, and seeded.

And that is what happened. An unexpected shake-up took place in Prokop's life, a gap opened up, and into it fell a seed.

The jolt occurred when he was told that Olbram was going off to live abroad. Marie was about to remarry and emigrate to her new husband's country, taking her son with her. Prokop was accustomed to being dealt unpleasant blows by fate, but this was one for which he was completely unprepared.

On the same day as he heard the news, Olbram came to stay with him. In the evening they had dinner as if nothing was amiss, neither of them daring to broach the subject. Afterwards they played a game of ludo.

When it was over and Olbram was resetting the pieces for a second game, Prokop got up, went to the bookshelves, and came back with an atlas. As he put it down on the table, he bumped into the game and knocked the pieces over. Then, trying hard to keep emotion out of his voice, he asked his son to show him the place where he would soon be going to live. Olbram swallowed the sweet in his mouth whole, opened the atlas, and leafed through it until he came to the map of the United Kingdom. He stopped, bent over the page, and examined it for a while. When he finally found the town he was looking for, he pointed at it with his sugar-sticky index finger, and uttered a name that sounded like a rumbling noise. Peterborough. He then reeled off everything he knew about it, as if it was a piece of homework he had learned by heart and didn't completely understand:

'It's here, do you see, it's in the Fens, they're marshes, and that river there is the Nene, it's not very far from the sea. There it is!'

Prokop saw nothing – except his son's very small finger – and a jumble of idiotic thoughts ran chaotically through his mind. It's not far from the sea but it's a very long way from Prague, I bet it rains the whole time in that god-awful country, it's bound to be deadly boring, what am I going to do without you, I'm going to be stuck here like a bloody old fool cleaning stairs, who am I going to tell stories to? And you won't see Olinka any more, you'll forget your sister and your father, you'll forget everything here, you'll become a foreigner, I don't want you to go, we won't be able to play ludo any more, the two of us won't be able to play anything at all, Peterborough, Peterborough, it sounds like a penal colony, I don't want you to go, the world is bare enough as it is, I need your childhood, you are my son, Peterborough, city of child thieves! No, I don't want you to go, you are my little boy . . .

Olbram, still engrossed in the map, was running his finger over England and saying the names of the towns, rivers and mountains, and above all the bays and estuaries. He was fascinated by the sea, which until now he had only seen in pictures and heard about in stories.

Prokop could still see nothing but that tiny, chubby finger, and as he gazed at its pink nail with a little sugar gleaming on the tip, a lump came to his throat. Olbram, who was almost ten, still had the soft, round hands of a very small boy; but from now on he was going to grow up far away, and as time went by his hands would grow longer, his fingers would loosen up and their gestures would become more relaxed. Prokop would no longer be able to see his son's hands, or hold them in his own. All the pain he felt at soon being separated from him and robbed of his childhood was concentrated on that clenched hand with the outstretched index finger.

What that finger was pointing to, as it jumped about from Norfolk to Dorset, from Essex to the Mersey Estuary, from the Wash to the Bristol Channel, was not a country, it was a landscape of disaster: of absence, of complete and utter remoteness. And all those seas around it were nothing but waters of ruin, loss and endless separation.

Olbram talked on and on in his chirpy voice, and had great fun making the red, green, yellow and blue plastic ludo pieces leap about all over England, then plop into the sea, at which point they became boats, reefs, sea monsters, lighthouses or sirens. But there was just one word pounding through Prokop's head: Peterborough, Peterborough.

Peterborough, a new name for misery. As if Prokop didn't have more than enough names for it already.

Olbram was going away. The Robinson-Radomír fresco on the bedroom wall would fade, the long beard with the decorated swirls would gather dust. From now on it was he, Prokop, who would be the melancholy castaway.

Olbram was leaving, and when he went, childhood would go away with him. Olinka had already left childhood behind; at nearly sixteen, she was past the age of games, dolls and stories. She had already embarked on the time of first loves and turbulent thoughts, and her visits to Prague were rare.

★

35

Somewhere in the depths of his being Prokop felt time teeter and sway, as if it were going to keel over in the slipstream of his son's departure, like an iceberg that drifts through arctic seas and then, when it moves into warmer waters and begins to melt at the base, loses its balance and suddenly capsizes, throwing up huge torrents of water amid a tremendous crash of breaking ice.

Prokop was already familiar with this dreadful feeling that time was collapsing and laying bare the anguish of solitude, separation and loss. There had been the death of his mother. He had seen her hardened, shrivelled body between the boards of the coffin before its lid was nailed shut. The sight was so appalling, so outrageous that it blinded him. He had a feeling of utter, sickly flatness and at the same time of the most intense shock. This was his mother, so familiar, so close, and yet it was not his mother, but an unknown being, a complete stranger. These two contradictory, irreconcilable, yet undeniable facts immediately threw him into a state of numbness. It was as if there was a very harsh light spurting up under his eyes, which was glaring with full force on to the mystery of existence, and in the same instant holding back, shedding no light on anything, but on the contrary intensifying the hard, stony mass of darkness all around. In fact the only thing that was made visible was the darkness itself.

His mother's body was already no more than a large piece of dried meat, which by now was lead-weighted with dark brown shadows.

Prokop felt the ground give way beneath him, as if it was the earth itself that was going to be buried. Time collapsed in a heap around him. The solidity and wholeness of his own body seemed diminished. In fact he was undergoing a mutilation; his roots were being severed. Now a raw opening gaped in him, through which death rushed in with a taste of rancid meat. And a wind whistled against his heart and howled out in the midst of his distress: 'It's *you* in the front line from now on.'

Then his sister died, and he found himself out there in the front line with no-one at all to keep him company.

But the months and years go by and pile up, the terror

subsides, and the grief grows easier to bear. Then comes forgetfulness, as thin and light as lichen on a rock, or pale grass waving on a sand-dune: but just enough to cover up the barren wastes and alleviate their harshness and dryness. And life goes on and reasserts its claim on us. Until another loss suddenly comes along. Then forgetfulness is rent asunder, the rock bursts, the sand heaves. The grasses and lichen, being too insubstantial, are destroyed. And underneath, grief lies intact, the untouchable face of the dead brushes against our own, and the tears which we thought had dried up for ever rise silently to full flood.

He had also been through that other ordeal of severance, when love is scorned and trust betrayed. Of all bereavements that is the ugliest; the unfaithful partner leaves like someone slipping out of the theatre in the middle of a bad performance, and for the one who is left alone the drama of abandoned love turns into a nightmare. When Marie left him, Prokop went to pieces; it was a sojourn in hell. Time seemed to flow on continuously, but in fact it had fossilised. The hours of the day were spiked with thorns on which he gashed himself with every step, every movement, every look. His mind was in torment, full to bursting with memories whose constant ebb and flow brought on sudden attacks of vomiting. As he swallowed his tears and choked back his cries of fury, pain, and appeal, he felt as if he were eating iron filings. He felt sick the whole time, and couldn't sleep; every night, Marie's body came back and lay beside him, an absent mass in the dark. He kept thinking that he could hear her voice and her breath in the room, but it was only the muffled, lonely sound of his own blood drumming insistently against his ears. It seemed as if her face, her smile and her shining, blue-green eyes were there again, right next to his shoulder. He reached out his hand, but it closed on a void. He tried by every possible means to gain control over this void and release himself from its power. Sleep did come in the end, but it didn't last long. His dreams took up arms against him, flushing out forgotten memories and playing back images so powerful that they wrenched him back into wakefulness. The images cried out under his eyelids. Over and over again Marie's body tore itself away from his own flesh. All night long Prokop was on a river that had burst its banks and was overflowing in all directions, with no land in sight and no ferryman to rescue him. He felt all the anguish of a castaway, tossed about on a raft somewhere in the storm, not even knowing what way to look for the land, or even if the land still existed. All he could do was wait: wait for daylight to come. At last it did come, but there was still no sign of land. Then all through the day he waited for night to fall. He waited against the flow of the tide, against the beat of time, to the point where he felt exhausted and sick, without even knowing what he was waiting for. He wished it was time for him to die, and there were even moments when he thought he was dying, when it seemed that he could no longer endure this horrible feeling of complete insecurity, of self-loathing, of utter greyness and flatness. The pain was unbearable. He had no control over it, he couldn't even give a name to it, and it was mortifying his flesh and his reason. But he didn't die; as usual, life hung on and refused to give in. People don't often die of grief, loss, failure or shame. They never die at the moment they choose. They struggle back on to their feet, a little older and heavier, and keep going as best they can, using whatever tricks they can to straighten up their lop-sided hearts. They can't declare that everything *is* all right, so they tell themselves instead that it *will* be all right. They start to conjugate their life in a new tense: not the present, but the indefinite future.

That evening, while Olbram was making the ludo pieces cavort along the coasts of England, Prokop was no longer telling himself anything. He was smoking, and looking at his son. He was huddling up deep in the heart of the present, putting off until later the torment of the separation to come.

When it was bedtime Prokop asked Olbram if he would like to sleep with him in his bedroom on the courtyard side. The child slid into the middle of the big bed. Before turning off the light, Prokop, sitting cross-legged on a pillow, told him a story.

2

'One day a young man arrived at the railway station in a large city, and got off the train with his luggage. He was very smart-ly dressed, which was hardly surprising, since he had come to ask his fiancée's parents for her hand in marriage. The parents had invited him to stay with them for a few days, just so that they could have a bit of time to look this future son-in-law over.

'What did seem rather odd was his luggage. He had three pieces: a small reddish-brown leather suitcase, which was very worn and tied shut with a strip of cloth, a large black metal trunk, and an oval hatbox covered in shiny old gold lacquer. The trunk was so huge and heavy that it was barely possible to lift it. It had little wheels, and the young man pulled it with a strap.

'The fiancée and her parents were waiting for the young man on the platform. All three of them were more than a little amazed to see what a strange collection of luggage he was dragging along with him. What's more, it wasn't long before the father began to get annoyed, because when he tried to put the trunk in the boot of the car he gave his back a nasty twist, and when he caught hold of the hatbox it flew out of his hands as if it had springs. Then once they got going his car would only crawl along the road at a snail's pace because of the enormous weight in the back.

' "What sort of a peculiar fellow is this?" muttered the father to himself at the wheel.

'The fiancée and her parents lived in a beautiful house sur-rounded by a garden, in the suburbs of the large city. The young man was shown to his room, and took his luggage up there straight away.

'After dinner, when the whole family was having coffee in the drawing-room and discussing the two young people's plans for the future, they began to hear strange murmuring sounds. There were even occasional little stifled laughs. One by one the parents and the fiancée gave a start, turned their heads like weather-vanes in a high wind and frowned, listening intently. As their conversation continued to be interrupted by these incomprehensible whisperings they lost the thread of it more and more, until they no longer knew what they were saying. That made the conversation a lot less boring than it had been before.

'Eventually the father spilt his cup of scalding coffee on his trousers. He jumped up with a yell. Faint chuckles could be heard round about. Furious, the father looked suspiciously at all the members of the family, but none of them had laughed.

' "You wouldn't happen to be a ventriloquist, would you?" snarled the exasperated father at the young man.

' "Sorry, that's a talent I don't possess," he replied, smiling.

'They all got up, said goodnight and went off to their own bedrooms. The young man locked himself into his. The fiancée, intrigued by what had happened in the drawing-room, crept up to the young man's bedroom and put her ear to his door. She had to hold back a cry of amazement.

'Her fiancé was talking very quietly in a foreign language, and other voices, lots of them, were answering him. They were the voices of men and women of all ages, and of children as well. The young man seemed rather angry; it was clear from the way he was speaking to the others that he was telling them off. There was lots of calling out and wailing, and they kept shushing one another to be quiet. The fiancée ran away, terrified. Who were all these people talking in secret, like robbers, to her fiancé? How had they got into the house? What were they plotting? Where had they come from? She ran and shut herself into her bedroom, and cried for a long time with her head buried in the pillows.

'The next day at breakfast, the parents, who had also slept badly, were astonished to see their daughter looking red-eyed and tired.

' "I think I've caught a cold," she said, and sneezed to make her lie seem more convincing. Immediately a little laugh was heard, and there were whispering and shushing noises around the table. Once again the parents and the fiancée twisted their necks in every direction, looked under the tablecloth and even in the sugar bowl, and lifted the lids of the jars and containers, but try as they might they could find nothing. Only the young man did not move, but he seemed embarrassed. He coughed slightly; the murmurings stopped.

' "Perhaps I've caught a cold too," he said. The father gave him a nasty look.

'It was a peaceful morning. The young man and his fiancée went for a walk in the garden.

'But no sooner had they taken three steps than the girl turned to her boyfriend and asked him: "Who on earth was with you in your bedroom last night?"

' "No-one."

' "You're lying! You were talking to some people, I heard voices, lots of voices of people I didn't know. Who were they?"

' "It was just me talking," said the young man. "I was talking to my memory."

' "Are you making fun of me? If you're not, my father must be right: you are a ventriloquist, and crazy into the bargain!" The young man smiled, the fiancée sulked.

'When they got back to the house, the mother was waiting for them on the steps. She looked very upset and extremely angry.

' "Young man," she hissed as soon as they started to climb the steps, "I assume you were just being absent-minded when you locked your bedroom door. It's not customary in this house to lock bedrooms, there's no thief in the family and we live in an atmosphere of complete trust! I wanted to tidy up a little in your room, just to be nice to you, and I couldn't get in!"

' "Here's the key," said the young man, taking it out of his pocket. "I do beg your pardon."

'The mother grabbed the key and turned her back on him; the daughter followed close behind her.

'Lunch went by without incident. But when it was time for

41

dessert, the mother, under the pretext of going to see if the pudding was baked in the oven, slipped away from the dining-room and shot straight up to her guest's bedroom. She inspected every nook and cranny in it, looked in the ward-robe, in the chest of drawers, behind the curtains and even under the bed. But she didn't notice anything unusual. Every-thing was in order. Then she went over to the luggage. At first she tried to open the big black trunk. But she couldn't, because it was padlocked.

' "No doubt about it," muttered the mother, "this fellow has some kind of obsession!" There was nothing she could do, so she turned her attention to the leather suitcase. It was not locked, so the mother could rummage in it to her heart's content. But she didn't find anything odd, just some under-wear and shirts. Only the hatbox remained. She undid the string around it and lifted the lid. A very foolish thing to do, as she was about to discover!'

Prokop broke off from his story to go and pour himself a glass of wine.

'What was there inside?' Olbram called out. 'A severed head?'

'No, something better than that.' Prokop came back with his glass in his hand, and went on.

'The box was empty. Completely empty. But it was full of voices. And as soon as it was opened, it let out a tremendous hubbub of words, sighs, shouts and whistling noises, all mixed up together. The mother leapt back, dropped the box and ran squealing out of the bedroom with her hands pressed to her ears.

'During this time the chocolate pudding had burnt in the oven and by now the smell was everywhere, not just in the kitchen but in the corridor and the dining-room too, and so everyone thought, when they saw the mother coming in with her head in her hands and moaning, that it was because her pudding was ruined.

'The mother slumped down on to her chair and exclaimed: "It's witchcraft! Witchcraft!"

' "No no," said her husband, "you just set the oven wrong, that's all."

'And of course the pudding was still in the oven. The fiancée got up and ran to the kitchen to take it out, and found that it was burned to a cinder.

'Soon there was a real din around the table; the mother was wailing, the father was bellowing, the fiancée let out a great yell because she had burned her hand on the red-hot dish, and on top of all that the clamour of the voices was growing louder and louder. In her flight the mother had set them all free and they had followed hot on her heels and had just swarmed into the dining-room. And they were having a whale of a time: guffawing, grousing, arguing away amongst themselves, humming, yawning, bursting out laughing. It was like being in the main room of a pub at closing-time. There was shouting and yelling going on all over the place.

'The mother was stamping her feet like a bad-tempered little kid and shrieking hysterically. The father emptied the water-jug over her head to calm her down. A roar of invisible laughter rang out. There were even some shouts of "Bravo! Bravo!" and a few whistles. The mother was sobbing now, her hair was completely ruined and water was dripping from her head; her make-up had run and her face was covered in black, blue and red streaks. She suddenly looked like a snivelling old clown. The young man felt sorry for her. The voices were choking with the hilarity of it all.

'The father began to run round the table, beating the air with his napkin or clapping his hands together, as if to crush the insolent voices. They just laughed even louder, and alternated their bravos with mocking "tut-tut!" sounds.

'In the end the father collapsed exhausted into an armchair. At last the young man, who until now had just sat still and said nothing, got up and said something which the parents did not understand. The voices fell silent. Even so there were a few "ooh!"s and other expressions of disappointment, but by and large they quietened down. Then the young man excused himself and left the room. As he went out his fiancée came in past him with her hand in a bandage.

'But no sooner had he returned to his room than the father, followed by the mother and daughter, burst in, armed with a hammer and a metal wedge. He walked straight over to the black trunk.

' "What are you going to do?" cried the young man.

'The father pushed him roughly out of the way and bellowed at him: "I'm going to open this metal monster, look in its belly and see what more black magic rubbish you're hiding in there!"

' "Don't do that!" exclaimed the young man. Whereupon the voices started up again, making more of a hullabaloo than ever. There was no laughter any more, just cries of anger and indignation, and also some moaning and groaning. "Ow ow ow! . . . boo hoo hoo! . . . oh oh! . . ."

'The mother and the fiancée, who were shaking with fear, tried one after the other to prevail upon the father not to attack the fearsome black trunk. But he was hell-bent. He started to bang on the lock of the trunk with all his might, and at the same time shouted to his wife to call the police, the fire brigade, the ambulance, the secret service, the exorcist. He was expecting the worst.

' "There's no need," said the young man. "But what you're doing is wrong. One must never do violence to beauty."

'The father was not listening to him; he was hammering on the lock, which eventually gave way. He lifted up the heavy lid. All the voices fell silent; only the father breathed a long "oh!" of amazement and admiration. Then the mother and daughter, clutching each other tightly, came over. As soon as they bent over the trunk they in their turn gave a deep "oh!" of wonder.

'The young man, still standing in the background, had lit a cigarette and was smoking and looking a little sad. As for the voices, they had crowded around the trunk and with one voice were going into raptures. Then they broke into a song, which was beautiful. Really very beautiful.'

Prokop broke off again and went to light a cigarette too, and to refill his glass. Then he came back to his son's side. Olbram asked him: 'Well, what happens this time? Is the trunk full of gazing eyes? Or smiles? Or smells?'

'Hmm,' said Prokop vaguely, suggesting he might be right. 'Just wait a bit. Look, I've blown three rings!' Three rings of bluish smoke rose above the bed.'

'Before I continue my story,' he added, 'you must sing me the song that the voices sang above the open trunk.'

'But I don't know what song they sang!' said Olbram.

'Neither do I. Sing the one you like best, one that you really enjoy.' Olbram thought for a moment, then began to sing. His singing was a little out of tune, but it was lovely all the same. When he had finished, Prokop continued his story.

'So there were all three of them, leaning over the trunk open-mouthed and wide-eyed, and the voices that were singing all around them no longer frightened or annoyed them, on the contrary. The fiancée even began to hum the tune softly.

'Bells rang, as if in answer to her humming. Then many other sounds started up.

'The buzz of a crowd, the noise of cars, the clanking of trams, seagulls' and ducks' cries, the wind in the leaves, the shouts of card players in cafés, the rumble of a train crossing an iron bridge, music being played at concerts, children kicking up a rumpus in school playgrounds . . . All the sounds of a city.

'For there was a real city in the trunk. A real city, with its streets and houses, its churches, its river, its bridges and boats, its parks, cafés, railway stations and museums, its birds in the trees and little old ladies on park benches, its castle on the hill, its cemeteries, shops and statues. And all its inhabitants. Its shopkeepers, pensioners, factory workers and lovers, its civil servants and soldiers, its strollers and nursery school children.

'And it was springtime. All the lilacs were in blossom, the apple trees, cherry trees and chestnut trees were a riot of pink and white. The streets, courtyards and parks were full of the sound of sparrows' song. And the straw-coloured light splashed on to window-panes and young girls' knees.

45

'And it was the end of summer. All the trees were russet, golden yellow and orangey, the hillsides were streaming with colour, and the gnarled branches of apple trees sagged under the weight of their fruit. And the ochre light shone like gold dust all along the pavements and on to young girls' bare feet.

'And it was the middle of autumn. The trees were half bare, the streets were strewn with leaves like gold and copper coins scattered in huge abundance by drunken pirates. And the wind was blowing hard; it smelt of rain, wet stone and coal. The light, tinged with mauve and violet, put rings round old people's eyes and on young girls' fingers.

'And it was winter. The trees were black, the roofs covered with snow. There were snowmen in the parks. The river was frozen. Rooks cawed, chimneys smoked in the lilac sky. The light was the colour of milk and the sun, as pale as a haystack, put a halo round young girls' ice-cold foreheads.

'It was an evening in May, the children were playing football in yards, the swans were tacking to and fro along the river.

'It was an afternoon in August, a thunderstorm was breaking out, the sky was lit up by flashes of lightning. Vesper bells were ringing out softly from church towers.

'And there was a great rainbow above the city. The wet pavements sparkled, as did the eyes of the people walking down the street.

'It was a fine Sunday in October, the children were running on a hillside, they were flying big kites of many different colours up among the clouds.

'It was a night in November. The cemeteries were full of fireflies that twinkled on the tombstones among large bouquets of purple and gold chrysanthemums, and wreaths of pine cones.

'It was Saint Nicholas' Day. Hordes of cherubs with fluttering tulle wings were prancing along the streets arm in arm with imps who had coal smeared on their faces, and . . .'

'Hey, how much longer is your story going to take?' Olbram interrupted him, yawning.

'OK, I'll hurry it up,' said Prokop. 'I'm going to zoom in and do a close-up shot:

'It was the end of the school day, and a little lad was running along with his satchel on his back; he hadn't done very well in class that day, but he had a few pennies in his pocket and he was dashing off to buy himself some sweets.'

Olbram, half asleep, opened one eye and added: 'And there was a big bloke sweeping the pavement with a fag in his mouth. He pinched one of my sweets and we went for a walk in the park.'

'Absolutely right,' said Prokop approvingly, and he took up the thread of his narrative once more.

'Then the young man went over to the trunk, took his fiancée by the hand and flew off with her into the Prague sky with all four seasons running through it. He took his fiancée into his memory, and showed her all the things he had loved as a child.

'The bandage around the girl's burnt hand came unwound. It unwound and unwound, like a fine white cloud rippling endlessly in the sky. It was her bride's veil. And where the burn had been, on her pale, trembling hand, a red rose opened up. It was flaming red, and had a spicy scent. It was her wedding ring. And the voices that had followed them murmured all around them, softly in the wind. And on top of Vinohrady Hill there was an old fellow sweeping the light, throwing up clouds of pink and golden dust.

' "I'd like you to meet my father," said the young man to his flying fiancée.'

Prokop fell silent. Olbram, stretched out across the big bed, had fallen asleep. His light, regular breathing accentuated the silence. Prokop watched him for a long time as he slept. Then he lay down fully clothed at the bottom of the bed, and with his legs curled up, his forehead resting against Olbram's knees, and his hands tucked round his ankles, went to sleep. His son's feet weighed gently on his chest. All night long a child's footsteps rang in his heart.

3

As the countdown to separation began, Prokop no longer felt that he was living in the present, but in a past that he would look back on in the future with nostalgia. Every time he was with Olbram he couldn't help thinking that the moments they were sharing now were already on their way to becoming part of that past. The slightest gesture, laugh or look from his son sparked off a strange emotion in him; it was as if this was both the first and last time that Olbram would move, speak, laugh or look at him.

Prokop would watch his son and think: 'He will have grabbed that apple, rubbed it against the sleeve of his pullover, taken a bite of it . . .; he will have opened his exercise book, I will have given him a dictation . . .; he will have done up the wrong buttons of his pyjama jacket with the yellow and red cherry print . . .' Movements, colours, shapes, smells and sounds burst open in Prokop's avid memory like huge ripe fruits falling to the ground with a muffled noise, closely followed by a sound of droning bees.

As the days went by, this inner fragmentation and dislocation of time became worse and worse. The present grew dilated, while the future and the past moaned quietly inside it in their toneless, haunting voices. Even when he was drinking and chatting with his friends in the Little White Bear, he would get an odd slipping, sliding feeling, and suddenly the drag he had just taken on his cigarette, the mouthful of wine he had just swallowed, or the piece of bread or cheese he was carrying to his mouth would take on a new, intense flavour.

The taste of the last cigarette, the final gulp of wine, the ultimate mouthful of food – but then what?

And yet life was still here, more dense and vivid than ever; he could feel it through every pore of his skin and in every fibre of his flesh.

Life was here, full of sound, movement and texture – only to fall silent and withdraw from him in the near future.

He would stand there in the hubbub of the room, fully present and attentive to everything that was moving and pulsating around him, with all five senses stimulated to the high-est point, and at the same moment he would feel himself being propelled into far-off time zones, cast out into the margins of the future, thrown back into a past that was soon to come. Out of this paradox grew others, and the more Prokop tried to remain vigilant and to take in every detail, the more abstracted he became. He was becoming absent through an excess of presence.

'Hey, Prokop, wake up!' his friends would call out when they saw him with that wild-eyed, faraway look. But he was not asleep, far from it; he was wearing himself out running a crazy marathon between the future and the past, right in the heart of the present. He was storing up every sensation, every second lived, in the vast warehouse of his memory. He was jumbling it all in any old how: the taste of food, voices, laugh-ter, the comings and goings of waitresses, the chinking of glasses, the movement and heat of bodies, the expressions on people's faces.

He didn't dare admit that to his friends, not least because he couldn't possibly have explained a phenomenon which he himself found so disconcerting. And so he smiled and joked, so as not to show how badly he was out of breath. You don't just suddenly become a long-distance runner over three time dimensions and get used to it overnight.

The only place where his mind didn't start to wander like this was the toilet. Here Prokop found some peace, and time finally came to rest for a while. It was when he was with other people, especially members of his own family, that he was most likely to experience the disquieting feeling that time was imploding. When he saw their faces and gestures, and listened to them speak and breathe, he was gripped by an intense feeling of the transience of the present. It was because he loved all these people and felt that he was tied to them by the numerous fibres and roots of affection, and because they all formed an integral part of his familiar landscape, that when he was with them he could feel time rushing by and see the shadow thrown by future absence trembling on the solid mass of the present. And he was also beginning to have the same feeling, although not so strongly, in all the places where he had been with other people in the past.

In the toilet he had always been alone; the seat of Prokop's household god was a haven for reading, dreaming and meditation, not melancholy. The flower of passing time on the ceiling grew blistered and puffy in the serenity of complete indifference.

Furthermore, Prokop took advantage of these moments of respite to reflect on the curious experiences he was having as a result of Olbram's imminent departure. He sensed that however painful they might be, they were bringing him very close to a revelation of vital importance. On the one hand they were commonplace; sooner or later everyone has the feeling that time is out of joint. But in his case they were so frequent and so intense that they were making him feel agitated and strange. And Prokop sensed that this was a strangeness of fundamental importance whose ins and outs he must explore, not just an oddity that could be put down to a passing disturbance of the senses.

He stopped reading in the toilet. He just sat there in the shade of the blue curtain, gazing at the whitish curls of smoke rising from his cigarette, the red glow of the tip, the soft fall of the ash. He was content to observe this flowing script, wordless yet eloquent, twirling upwards in milky arabesques through the half-light of the shrine. Sometimes he followed one of the wan curls with his fingertip; the smoke disintegrated, and with it Prokop's thoughts.

Just as the runes of the *Kalevala* had done, this elusive alphabet threw Prokop into a very mild disarray which left his thoughts hanging in mid-air and sowed in him seeds of astonishment, infinite desire, and deep humility.

But as yet there was no sign at all of inspiration.

One morning Prokop passed Mr Slavík on the stairs. It was the time when he normally carried his old dog downstairs in his arms. But the big man's hands were empty, his arms were dangling heavily by his sides, and he was wearing the long puppeteer's scarf round his neck. His eyes were as red as his scarf. Prokop stared fatuously at him, but Mr Slavík avoided his eye and hurried on down the stairs.

4

The time came for Olbram to leave. Prokop and he spent their last day together quietly. Olinka was there too, and the three of them went for a walk through Petřín park. They climbed up to the Observation Tower, then Olbram said he felt like seeing the maze of distorting mirrors again. They wandered along the corridor, zigzagging through warped reflections of themselves in which they were all flattened and squat one minute and then absurdly tall and spindly the next. There were lots of children there; the maze was teeming with restless, rowdy monsters.

A little girl of three, perched on her father's shoulders, burst into tears when she saw herself with a giraffe's neck, an ostrich's head and two enormous protruding eyes, and her father suddenly transformed into a dwarf with elephant's calves.

Then they went back down the hill along damp paths from which bitter-sweet odours of bark, moss and humus arose, heralding the arrival of autumn.

As his children went on ahead, Prokop watched the supple way they walked, or rather skipped because of the steep slope. But there was something new now in Olinka's bearing; it was that sense of power which exudes from young girls' bodies, a mixture of insolence and modesty, innocence and wildness, desire and grace. As the city's roofs turned the colour of rust in the setting sun, Olinka's shoulders towered over them, the swaying of her hips lent grandeur to that of the trees in the gardens and terraced orchards down below, her bare legs accentuated the brightness of the river and her long blond plait shimmered with gold and copper lights. For a moment the sun rested on her shoulder, the purple glow of the twilight

51

trembled in the hollow of her neck, and then the sun rolled along her arm and fell into the river. On she went with her sauntering step, like a circus performer juggling with the clouds, the light, the domes and towers, with the wind and the birds. Olbram was prancing about beside her; the first dead leaves were being blown off the trees and swirling around them. The two children were dancing the dance of twilight, of the end of summer, up on the heights of the city.

They dined early in a restaurant near the embankment. At the end of the meal Olinka gave her brother a royal blue scarf and an address book in which she had coloured in all the letters. Prokop gave his son a watch, a key-ring with a metal whistle attached to it, and a little compass inside a midnight blue plastic box. Olbram was full of wonder, and so deeply moved that he wanted to give his sister and father something too. But it had to be something big, really beautiful, unforgettable. Something that couldn't be lost or used up. He thought for a moment and looked all around him, then suddenly he had an inspiration.

'To you,' he said to Olinka, 'I give that cloud, you see, the one that's passing above the castle over there, the little one that's a bit pink and orange. Every time there's a cloud that colour in the sky, it'll be for you, just you and nobody else. And to you papa, I give the moon. The whole of the moon; every time it's full it'll be for you. This way you'll never be able to lose my presents, or break them.'

The little orangey-pink cloud was slowly drifting across the sky; by now it was floating above the tower of St George's Basilica. Olinka followed it with her eyes, not looking away for a second. As for the moon, it was only just beginning to show through, as yet very pale in the slate-grey sky.

And at the same time it was rising in Prokop's heart. Like the little girl who had taken fright in the maze, Prokop at that moment believed what he saw and was taking what he was told quite literally. Olbram was giving him the moon, and he was receiving it as he would have done a very precious, fragile object, handling it with gestures of great delicacy.

All this was happening invisibly, inside him; it was as if

52

transparent, ethereal hands had just come to life and spread open all around his heart, and were now busily smoothing out his thoughts and his memory, stretching them until they were as high and wide as the sky.

The moon needs space, a vast, smooth expanse of it, and much height and room for movement. It needs silence and contemplation. Its trajectory is long, its brightness so frail that it can very easily be lost from sight.

Prokop felt an urgent need to make sure, unstintingly and without delay, that he received with the utmost care this gift which his son had just presented to him. It was a vast, absolute gift, of significance acute beyond measure, such as only little children can give when they feel love and want to express it. They possess nothing in their own right, and in any case there are no riches which for them could equal the infinite expanse of feeling that swells in their soul; so they go and search right across the universe, and from all the things they see there and all the mysteries they find, they pluck the impossible and offer it up to you with a smile of purest innocence, as if it were an orange or a daisy. To them, this seems only natural. With their bare hands, without flourishes or fancy speeches, they give you the bronze gleam of the ocean, the passage of a shooting star, a frost pattern or a night-bird's song. They give you the beauty of the world, never suspecting the measure of terror that it harbours within it. They give you their trust, not realising the heavy, acute burden of responsibility that this places upon you. There are some adults who still have this child-like seriousness and supreme artlessness when they fall deeply in love; for them, the absolute in love is a matter of life and death. To betray them is to steal the world from them, to turn their days into a long mortal agony. Prokop's sister Romana had died of a grief like that.

The time came to say goodbye to Olbram. It would be many long months, one or two years even, before Prokop saw his son again. But, with the same tiny, chubby finger he had used to point to that new name for misery, Peterborough, Olbram had also shown the place where a faithful, luminous memory

53

could always be found. Prokop had received the gift of the moon. And as a result, the hectic time race of the last few weeks stopped, and the painful upheavals it had inflicted on Prokop were over at last. Time settled back to normal, and the present came to rest for a while.

Every time the full moon rose, Olbram's childhood would become fully visible, near-white and gentle, and likewise, every time an orangey-pink cloud passed on the horizon, Olinka's youth would blow on the earth like a breeze tasting of ivy and fresh grass. Cloud and moon would henceforth be mirrors more fabulous than those of the Petrín maze. They would reflect the whole earth, its cities, seas and forests; they would echo Prokop's solitude, purging him of all bitterness, and surround the children's absence with such a halo of dreams and tenderness that their presence would shine through it, clearer than before.

They would transform the shape of things, and restore them to their proper proportions. They would be sources of second light.

And because of them, a different light would be thrown on everything, all around, from now on.

THE BEAUTIFUL ELSEWHERE
IN THE HERE AND NOW

1

Prokop's heart had been thoroughly shaken up and knocked about, and his thoughts had been turned over and thrown in every direction. In the midst of all this confusion, however, a seed had been sown.

Just a little seed, nothing at all really; but when your life is as barren as Prokop's was in his pariah days, even the smallest things count for a lot.

His desert was lit up by the moon.

It might have gone no further than that: a moonbeam shining on a dull patch of grey. The seed might have dried up.

But it didn't; it germinated.

What enabled it to do so was a series of encounters of various kinds, almost all of which were apparently quite commonplace or even completely insignificant. There were people he met, for instance, who left their mark on him in new ways. Some were strangers he passed in the street, others close friends he suddenly saw in a new light. Encounters with books still took place, of course, behind the blue curtain in the toilet.

Books and people, words and faces, the shifty eyes of a passer-by, something interesting he happened to read, or a look or gesture he secretly intercepted; all these trivial little occurrences, at first sight so unconnected, intermingled to create a clearer atmosphere and a favourable climate for the flowering of rêverie and the imagination.

Prokop, his eyes quite iridescent with moonlight, was more than ever willing to be carried along by the wind of encounters: a wind of chance and wonderment.

And as a result the quality of the light shining on the world around him began to change, as if the light of day were slightly infused with the light of the moon. An ivory or silvery gleam

trembled in the air and coated everything with a slight suggestion of uncertainty. It wasn't time now that was splitting apart
within and drifting off in opposite directions, it was light. And
under this double illumination the whole visible world,
beginning with human bodies and faces, was transfigured.
And Prokop's ideas of what was beautiful or ugly, commonplace or rare, were no longer confined within the straitjacket
of habit and convention.

The first person Prokop suddenly saw with his new eyes and
in this new light was none other than himself. And once again
it happened in the toilet.

He had just put down the newspaper, having skimmed
through a few articles in it. It was always the same old story,
here a war, there a disaster, either man-made or natural,
somewhere else a hostage-taking, an assassination, or a coup
d'état. The financial and political pages were the usual hotch-
potch of lies, empty phrases and dirty dealings in high places.
There was scandal and corruption in the West, bankruptcy
and petty tyranny in the East, poverty and famine in the
South. Not to mention all the things that were left unsaid
and unadmitted. The chronicle of an ordinary day in the
world.

Feeling the need for a little light relief, Prokop leant over to
get a cigarette and his lighter and to pick out one of the
comics that Olbram had left behind. And it was at that
moment that he saw himself – sitting there on the toilet seat,
with his trousers crumpled round his ankles, a few sparse red
hairs on his legs, and a large beer belly which was threatening
to burst two buttons on his shirt.

He had caught sight of himself like this thousands of times,
but whatever he might have said about it in the Little White
Bear on the evening of the discussion about the household
gods, he hadn't really paid much attention before now.

What Prokop saw today was no different from usual, and
yet he was shocked. Not because at that moment he noticed
what a big paunch he had and how slack his muscles were –
he wasn't in the least concerned about that – but because all

of a sudden the laughableness of his own condition leapt to his consciousness like a cat jumping on to someone's shoulders with all its claws out.

It wasn't even to do with him, Prokop Poupa, personally; it was more than that. What was suddenly and with utmost plainness revealed to him was the condition of the strange human animal of which he was but a commonplace specimen among several billions of others: a great protozoon, overblown and puffy, which in the course of its development had become tragically complicated and corrupt in the extreme. Prokop's eyes gaped in utter astonishment, and his mind was in turmoil.

There he sat looking down at his voluminous, pallid belly, with a packet of Spartas in one hand and his lighter in the other, and an icy void swirling around inside him. After he had been in this stupor for quite a while, he felt some words welling up within him, from a distant source but with great commotion, like blood rushing violently to the heart at a moment of terror. They were the words of a poem by Bedrich Bridel which he must have learned many years before, perhaps in his youth. Now suddenly its lines with their accents of torment came spiralling up from deep in his memory.

> You — sweetness, I — poison,
> You — delight, I — bitterness,
> I am ugliness, You are beauty,
> I am wrath and You are glory,
> I am vile and You are pure,
> I am strife, You are victory,
> What am I but cesspit and mire?
> Worth less than a feather in the wind,
> And less than the wind itself,
> More fickle than dust,
> Or powder that flits in the air.
> I am bloated scum,
> Most exalted in joy
> But when there is sudden change
> My heart is made sick by misfortune.

59

What made Prokop's spirit sick was the absurd, and what filled his heart with disgust was the worthlessness of his poor being. His eyes remained fixed on his paunch and his bunched-up trousers. The poem continued to unwind the bizarre coils of its litanies into the silence of the toilet.

> *I am a hundred times more horrible*
> *Than purulent ulcers,*
> *Manure or dung,*
> *I am quite fetid and pale,*
> *Uglier than plague or poison,*
> *No better than an ulcer, a rotting carcass,*
> *Dung, stench, violent poison*
> *Giving scabies to the obscene body.*

The obscene body! These words rang out like a peal of thunder in Prokop's brain. On the one hand he was shocked by the outrageousness of the words, but on the other he felt that behind this immoderate language a truth was being proclaimed. The obscenity in question was not so much a matter of immodesty as of a great, pitiable wretchedness. A wretchedness of the whole being, cramped within the blubber of stupidity and the lard of cowardice: of the spirit gone flabby through indolence, and of the heart grown impotent through egotism.

The obscene, opaque body in which the soul has stifled, now reduced to a great piece of machinery functioning for itself alone. A body which, however graceful its outward form may appear, is nonetheless hatching within it the vermin which will soon teem in its cadaver.

> *I am a pool of sin*
> *I am nothing but rottenness,*
> *A worm, a stinking cesspool,*
> *Vice, woe and treachery . . .*

A violent gurgling sound shook the plumbing and interrupted the flow of Bedrich Bridel's lamentations. Fellow tenant Slavík had just pulled the chain. Prokop stood up, pulled up his trousers, and flushed his own toilet with one sharp pull on the string, thus sending a further echo of the rumblings of deluge on down into the Sluneckos' apartment. Then, perturbed by the snatches of Bridel's long poem that were irrupting into his memory, he rushed to his bookshelves and rummaged among his books. It took quite a long search before he unearthed the work. Then he went into his bedroom and settled down to read.

Outside the light was fading; a fine icy rain was falling from the dull grey sky and trickling down the bare trees. Muffled music was coming up from the church-warehouse, where the organist was diligently rehearsing a Bach chorale. Slender columns of brown smoke rose from the chimneys. Prokop was so absorbed in his reading that he didn't even bother to get up from his armchair to switch on the light. As he read in the half-darkness, bending over with his face very close to the book, his mind became tangled up in the wreathed columns of verse through whose rambling twists and turns Bedrich Bridel pursued his anguished enquiry into man's condition and at the same time celebrated the glory of God.

It was a dizzy whirl between grace and sin, wonder and dereliction, pure light and deepest darkness. And the images swirled, one moment in colours of mud, soot, blood, ashes and pus, the next in shades of purple, honey, dew, gold and clear sky.

Here was the obscene, wretched body – savagely contorted, its folds and recesses full of dark shadows and purulent matter, and yet wound all around by a fine convolvulus streaming with light.

And therein lay an essential paradox; the obscene body, that gnarled trunk bristling with thorns and cankers, did not find solace in the tender embrace of the gentle convolvulus, but suffered from it.

It was almost dark when Prokop reached the last lines, so humble and simple at the conclusion of this torrent of brutal, resonant images.

A little worm crawling on the earth,
I offer up this nothing in the darkness!

Prokop closed the book. Given his character and the way his life had gone, he had no difficulty at all in agreeing with the penultimate line. That he was no more than a pot-bellied worm dragging itself painfully along the ground, he scarcely doubted. But between the penultimate line and the last one there was a gaping chasm. 'I offer up this nothing in the darkness!'

How was he to offer up his own nothing, his stale, dreary uselessness, in the darkness and silence? Olbram for his part had not troubled himself with such questions on the evening when he had given a cloud to his sister and the moon to his father. He had plucked two beautiful fruits from the visible world and given them just as they were, thus endowing them with real weight.

Prokop, burdened by fifty-four years packed with failure and doubt, felt incapable of carrying out such a feat: seizing the unseizable, making the impossible bear fruit. How could he offer himself as a gift when he was nothing? For a start, that was an image of nonbeing; it wasn't linked to any form, it didn't belong to the visible world. And then, above all, to whom was he to make this gift? To that stranger called God? To that great unknown quantity?

The fact was that Prokop had never taken up a precise position as regards the existence of God. When it came down to it he could not have said whether he was a believer or a non-believer. He floated in a marginal area, undecided and quite possibly not caring very much, for he had never actually explored the subject in depth, even if he had sometimes had occasion to hold forth on it.

That was why his astonishment that evening knew no bounds. It was not just the meaning of the little phrase, 'I offer up this nothing in the darkness', that disconcerted him; he was surprised by the very fact that a question of this type could have stopped him so abruptly in his tracks.

Up until then the various emotional experiences that he

had had from reading had always been of the literary sort, and it was primarily his imagination that they had aroused. Now for the first time his agitation was of a different kind, touching a part of him which had hitherto remained in limbo. His imagination, far from being set in motion, was completely obliterated. The astonishment he felt brought no dazzling images along with it; on the contrary it filled his spirit with a sort of harsh grey roughcast. It was no longer a matter of playing with words, of letting their harmonies and symmetries resonate in his mind, of taking delight in images and visions, of venturing into the depths of the visible world as if into the wings of a magic theatre. No, the theatre was empty, wings and stage formed one single space plunged into semi-darkness, and there was a cold wind quietly howling in the prompter's box.

Nothing he had read had ever had such an effect on Prokop before. It was a new experience, bitter and dry; the words engendered neither echoes nor dreams of any kind.

A line of poetry, a simple little line had at one stroke wiped out the whole of language and broken the spirit of play and make-believe. Prokop felt that he had hit rock-bottom where language and thought were concerned.

And all because he had happened to bend down over his great beer belly! All because a nonsensical association of ideas had led him straight from the contemplation of his fat paunch to the sudden recall of a poem buried in a hidden recess of his memory. It was quite simply ridiculous.

'I must say,' thought Prokop as he got up from the armchair to go and put on the light at last, 'that joke about the household god living in my loo is beginning to turn sour!'

He was perplexed. When thoughts come to you out of the blue it isn't always easy to weigh them up and judge what they are made of. Is it incense or sulphur, or maybe just dust?

Whatever it was made of, the little sentence continued to drill into his brain as forcefully as ever. 'I offer up this nothing in the darkness!'

2

Grotesque though it might seem, something as run-of-the-mill as the observation of his pot-belly was enough to trigger off a whole revolution in Prokop's mind. It was a revolution devoid of colour or sound; whereas normally his mind was only too quick to career off aimlessly into all sorts of day-dreams that were not only highly colourful but full of sound to boot, now it remained entirely free of phantasmagoria and wild poetic-philosophical imaginings. This was an exceedingly sober, discreet internal revolution. But it also had exceedingly deep roots.

Prokop Poupa had never had a very high opinion of himself, not at least since he had reached adulthood. Early on he had grasped the sheer extent of people's stupidity and vanity, and far from looking down on them, he had recognised that he was no different from the rest. Later, when he was reduced to sweeping the pavements and washing his fellow-citizens' stairs, he was also able to rid himself once and for all of any remaining vestiges of pride and self-regard. Only very occasionally did he suffer a slight relapse.

But now he had just gone a step further in this process of distancing himself from his own being; or perhaps it was more a matter of putting himself in a different perspective. Suddenly he saw himself through new eyes. They were sharper and at the same time more naïve. They were also tactile, and they were groping around in the darkness.

With one stroke he had pierced through the substance of his flesh and felt the weight of his body: not his physical body, which any bathroom scales could tell him weighed around sixteen stone, but the weight of his existence. It wasn't possible to put a figure on it, since it tipped the scales towards negative infinity. This breakaway plunge into nothingness threw his mind into complete confusion; he no longer understood anything about himself. He was like a little child who discovers a strange new insect that is clumsy and misshapen. What is this ridiculous, disturbing creepy-crawly? Does it slither, scurry, flit, splash or hop? Does it sting, bite, suck or claw? Will it harm you or not? Does it sing, screech or chirp? Is its shell tough or fragile? Supposing it's a bit of all of these at once?

Yet this disquieting little creature must have a reason for existing. Prokop Poupa, the large creature, was in terrible doubt about it all.

With his new-found expert eye for abnormalities in the insect world, Prokop soon began to see everything else differently as well. In particular he began to perceive things and people from a new angle, which sometimes made their shape, size and height appear fantastically distorted. A visit he made to his friend Aloïs Pípal around this time gave him the opportunity to test out this disconcerting optical disturbance.

Whenever Prokop went to see Aloïs, his friend always did him the honour of playing what he called 'the big game', that is to say that he ran all his electric trains for him. This never failed to give Prokop enormous pleasure, especially since Aloïs kept rearranging his track and adding new touches to the scenery around it.

It was a huge railway system which took up the whole living-room floor, and in order to move about in it one had to tiptoe round with the most extreme caution. Networks of rails meandered among a wonderful landscape of cardboard mountains covered with white gloss-paint snow and hills planted with forests of dried thistles, feathers and dwarf cactuses. Villages with painted wooden houses and churches stretched out over the hillsides and valleys. Small towns and hamlets were connected by winding paths covered in sand or fine stones. There was even a miniature lake in an oval dish which was deep enough for some tiny fish to swim in.

Then there were the stations, five in all, in differing sizes and styles, all made by Aloïs in painted or roughcast plate. The most beautiful was the one he had built to look exactly like the station at Vysehrad. There in front of it, in a pose which suggested rather ludicrously that it was on guard duty, stood the same statue of a white lion, and around it were the same half-bare, poorly-tended patches of garden with little wooden huts stuck right down at the far end.

The most eyecatching was Hrabal, named after the writer in honour of his novel *Closely Watched Trains*. To illustrate this book Aloïs had of course chosen the scene where the charming telegraphist Zdenicka shows her bare buttocks, copiously decorated with the official rubber-stamp marks that Hubicka the sub-stationmaster has applied to them. So there in the middle of the platform was a little doll with no pants on, showing off her shapely, date-stamped behind.

Aloïs' railway world was peopled by many other characters as well. He changed his figurines according to the seasons. Now for instance, as it was the beginning of December, he had dotted about the countryside a whole host of little angels and imps to mark the feast of Saint Nicholas. Next to the white lion at Vysehrad station, the place normally occupied by the station-master had been taken by a cherub in a pale pink crêpe paper robe with pretty wings made of tiny goose feathers. In his hand this cherub-railwayman carried his halo as a lamp. Another angel, flanked by two imps with horns and large crimson eyes, sat astride a level crossing. Soon the imps would be banished from the railway landscape; they belong to Saint Nicholas' entourage, but not to that of the Three Kings. Only the angels would remain, and a horde of Christmas figures would invade the scene when Aloïs transformed the track, as he did every year, into an enormous crib. That was when Aloïs' railway craze reached its apotheosis; waves of sheep, led by shepherds, angels and peasant women, snaked up and down the hills, there were gold and silver forests all over the mountains, goats and ewes rubbed shoulders with the camels of the Three Kings come from far in the East, hens pecked at the stars that were scattered all over the ground, and just for once Zdenicka the doll had her pretty pink backside covered with a lace petticoat. Vysehrad station was temporarily doing duty as a holy stable and the white lion stood alongside the ox and the ass, watching with them over the little straw-filled cradle.

On Christmas evening Aloïs put all his trains into operation. The Virgin Mary arrived in a flaming red miniature old locomotive, Saint Joseph came in on the Orient Express, there were clusters of angels, old women wearing scarves and carrying baskets of eggs, shepherds with their arms raised in ecstasy, fiddlers and fife players, all piling one on top of the other on to the wagons of goods trains. As for the Infant Jesus, he made his solemn appearance in a yellow maintenance truck. Aloïs orchestrated the comings and goings of all these trains as they swept past each other, roared up mountains, plunged into tunnels and pulled their brightly-coloured little carriages across the candle-lit countryside. For more than a fortnight all his friends' children came to his home to admire the spectacle, which he never wearied of starting up again. This year for the first time Olbram would not be among them.

That day when Prokop went to see him, Aloïs told him about his latest stroke of inspiration. He had decided to put little bells into each of the seven churches that were scattered over the hills and valleys, and also into the keep of the fortress which overlooked the goldfish lake. He planned to make the bells ring out one by one on Christmas Eve, so that the Holy Child's maintenance truck would arrive in Vysehrad to a great shower of tinkling notes.

Prokop, squatting down beside a mountain, was listening to his friend and at the same time following the movements of the trains with his eyes. He felt like Gulliver in Lilliput, or Pantagruel transported forward into the century of electricity.

The telephone rang in the next room. Aloïs got up and left the living-room. Prokop remained alone in the middle of the railway. One by one the trains slowed down then stopped, except for one black and green engine which continued to fly along the rails.

Far from disturbing the silence, the gentle hum intensified it. There was something enchanted about this plaster and cardboard landscape. It made Prokop think of the passage in Book Four of *Pantagruel* where Rabelais tells of the giant's strange boat journey into a land of ice where the air is full of frozen words that look like sugared almonds and give out the sounds of various voices as they melt. In the same way the humming engine was carrying around translucent pearls with reedy little sounds curled up inside them.

Now it must be said that if a man weighing about sixteen stone sits on his hunkers next to a miniature landscape with the whole mass of his body hanging over mountains, churches, railway stations and a throng of people, it's hardly surprising that he should feel like Pantagruel, and that his sense of proportion should go awry for a moment. But in Prokop's case, tormented as he was all the time now by the expression 'obscene body', the feeling was so unsettling that it made his head swim.

The Christmas figures had not yet swarmed in to worship and adore; the landscape was still populated entirely by angels as light as frost flowers and swarthy devils with rats' tails, amidst whom the cheeky telegraph operator stuck her rubber-stamped bottom in the air, as if to say to all and sundry, 'I don't give a damn!'

But what was it that this little cutie with the cheeky backside didn't give a damn about? Was it the singing of the angels or the cries of the demons, or perhaps the passengers in the trains? It was the whole earth, heaven and hell, eternity, and good and evil alike.

Prokop stared aghast at Zdenicka's buttocks, just as he had peered at his own potbelly. And once again he was plunged to the depths of an abyss. It was as if he was touching, with the tip of his tactile gaze, the watery flimsiness of his own being.

And yet it was not completely worthless, this being, any more than the telegraph operator doll's rump was. But just like her he had gone through life blithely not giving a damn – and about what? About his own salvation.

Salvation! The word sprang from nowhere and invaded his consciousness, just as the word God had done the other day. Where on earth did these dreadful, mind-boggling words come from? Was it from the green and black engine, puffing breathlessly along there with its cargo of humming, translucent pearls?

68

Prokop let his eyes wander over the Lilliputian landscape stretching out at his feet, and at the same time his pallid thoughts wandered through the deserts of doubt that were opening up in his mind. Because everything went hand in hand with its opposite; the extremely small called out to the infinitely large, the trivial to the sacred, and the grotesque to the solemn. Everything went with something else, and nothing stood to reason on its own. The doll's bare buttocks imprinted a fearsome question mark on Prokop's consciousness. He felt lost; his world of habit was falling apart, the landmarks he was accustomed to were disappearing fast, the few certainties he had hung on to were being overturned. And he was discovering that everything he had managed to do and think until that day was inadequate, mere dust and froth, and that the most important things remained unaccomplished. He would have to go back to square one. But what was that, where was it, and how was he to do it?

What on earth had been going on of late? wondered Prokop, bewildered. A glance falling at the wrong moment on to his abdominal blubber had thrown him into a state of consternation, then carried him off into a swirl of gloomy reflections on the meaning and destiny of mankind. And now, right out of the blue, the sight of a doll with a jolly backside was causing him spiritual anguish. The fantasy he had improvised one evening with his friends was backfiring; he was thoroughly anxious about it, and wondered how much further it was going to go. Could it be that those nice household gods that they had all invited to live in their homes, whether in the kitchen, cellar, balcony or toilet, actually existed? Could they have heard the call and leapt swiftly into action? But who exactly were these invisible spirits of places anyway? Far from bringing peace and protection to the abode, they seemed rather to be amusing themselves by introducing alarm and confusion into it. They were making everyday, familiar things seem strange and outlandish, turning humour into panic, and making it impossible to distinguish between the real and the imaginary, or between time and eternity.

Salvation: what did it consist of, what could it possibly mean? Why on earth was this question which he had never asked himself in more than half a century of existence now suddenly worming itself into his mind?

When Aloïs came back into the living-room carrying two opened bottles of beer, he found Prokop on all fours, with his belly crushing the tops of the mountains, his hands shakily holding him up above the fields, and his eyes riveted on the doll's buttocks. Aloïs laughed at him.

'You're worse than the children,' he said. 'As soon as they spot my Zdenicka they can't take their eyes off her stamped bottom, and every time they come I have to tell them the story of the sub-stationmaster and the telegraph operator all over again.'

'I know,' agreed Prokop, rising to his feet with some difficulty, 'as a matter of fact you tell the story so well that you've put some really terrific ideas into Olbram's head. One day the stupid idiot got hold of a girl in his class and covered her buttocks with transfers of little pigs. The kid's mother gave me hell.'

They sat down on the sofa and drank their beer while the trains roared off again along the rails. Fine snowflakes were beginning to fall outside the window. Aloïs got straight on to his favourite subject, the theatre. He always came back to his favourite authors, Chekhov and Shakespeare. The last time he had gone on stage, about twenty years before, he had played Uncle Vanja, and since then he had been obsessed with this character. By dint of going over and over poor old Vanja's lines he had ended up making them his own. His wife Marketa even maintained that he often shouted out Uncle Vanja's speeches in his sleep at night. But for some time now he had been haunted by another character: King Lear.

'I'm the right age for the rôle,' Aloïs would say, ruffling his white hair, 'and above all I feel it, I feel it!' He knew the text by heart.

''It's true,' Marketa confirmed, 'he's changed his nocturnal repertoire, but now that he's a mad king there's no peace at all. And when he isn't declaiming, he's snoring!'

Outside the snow was still falling, and a chalky light shone into the living-room where Aloïs, who would never play King Lear, went on and on rehearsing the speeches he loved.

> *Blow, winds, and crack your cheeks! rage! blow!*
> *You cataracts and hurricanoes, spout*
> *Till you have drenched our steeples, drowned the cocks!*
> *You sulphurous and thought-executing fires,*
> *Vaunt-couriers to oak-cleaving thunderbolts,*
> *Singe my white head! (. . .)*

3

One morning in January, as he was sweeping snow off the pavement, Prokop noticed a little old woman jumping up and down in front of a bottle bank a little further down the street. The threadbare black coat she was wearing had gone greeny-bronze with age, and its collar was trimmed with yellowing fur. Wisps of white hair, as faded and yellowish as the rabbit-skin collar, straggled untidily out from under her woollen bonnet. Her clumpy shoes seemed far too big for her feet, despite the many pairs of socks she had on under them, which were bunched up in great rolls round her ankles.

Hanging by one hand on to the edge of the large skip, the old woman was desperately trying to reach down to the bottom of it and get hold of something. But she couldn't manage it, because she was too small; the poor old thing was all shrivelled up, and looked as if her bones were even more fragile than the bottles and jars inside the skip.

'Jesus and Mary! Jesus and Mary!' Prokop heard her sigh in tones of real distress, but she kept on trying, unable to resign herself to failure. Prokop propped his wooden rake against the wall and went over to ask if he could help.

Without even turning round to look at him, she pointed to the object of her desire, and said in a beseeching voice, 'Oh

71

yes please! I'd like to get that mirror out, that one there. It's not even broken!'

Prokop bent over and pulled out the mirror from among the pieces of broken glass.

'Be careful! Don't hurt yourself! Jesus and Mary!' squealed the old woman, clasping her hands.

Prokop held out the mirror.

'Oh my Lord!' she exclaimed, clapping her hands in glee like a little girl, 'it's all in one piece!'

So it was, but it was flecked all over with black spots. She took it in her hands with infinite caution.

For a moment she stood still and looked down at the mirror, radiant with joy. It was not her own reflection that she found so enchanting; no doubt it was a very long time indeed since she had paid the slightest attention to her own face with its many wrinkles, liver spots and downy hairs. She was looking at herself without seeing herself. Her gaze was penetrating much deeper than her mere reflection, or rather going off to a different place altogether: not to the world of memory, but to an elsewhere that exists here, in the visible and immediate present. A beautiful elsewhere showing through on the surface of the visible world and radiating a childlike joy.

It was so cold that the mirror quickly became misted up by the old woman's breath. She took a handkerchief out of her pocket and wiped off the mist, which formed again almost immediately. She wiped it again. While this was happening Prokop stood still as well, despite the icy cold. He was looking at the old woman deep in contemplation of the mirror, and watching the way the mist quickly formed and then, when it was wiped off, the reflection reappeared and then misted over again. And it seemed to him that the reflection was becoming more and more transparent, and that at the same time the old woman's face was becoming clearer as well. Not that it was losing its wrinkles and blemishes, or starting to grow young again – it was still the face of an old woman who couldn't care less about her pitiful appearance – but it was being trans-

72

figured. A glow was rising into it and illuminating it from within. And the old woman was becoming transparent.

Although Prokop was chilled to the bone he did not make the slightest movement, didn't even shuffle his feet. He was studying the old woman, fascinated by the translucence which was gradually stealing over her. He was seeing her as all individuals are perhaps perceived after they die, in the absolute nakedness of their being.

Suddenly all the confused questions that had been troubling Prokop for a while came rushing back to him in full force. Once again he saw his ventriloquist paunch, heard its voluble poetic rumblings, and saw the bare-bottomed doll on the cardboard station platform, surrounded by angels and demons. It was like a jigsaw puzzle or a guessing game with pictures instead of words. The pieces, however oddly shaped they seemed, were starting to fit together. It was clear that the 'obscene body' was simply the body turned in on its own flesh and therefore craving nothing but physical ease, pleasure and agreeable or even intoxicating sensation: gorged on the satisfaction of its egotistical desires, wholly preoccupied, depending on its age, with its own beauty, power, charm, and health; so wrapped up in itself that its soul, turned opaque, no longer gave off the slightest spark of reflected light. It was a body which set itself up as a self-sufficient whole, completely shut off and fossilised, and offering the enjoyment of this separate entity to no-one but itself.

'Look at me! Admire me! Desire me! Pamper me!' it cried out to other people, treating them merely as mirrors designed to enhance its own beauty. The obscene body was all aquiver with vanity and greed, it gravitated around its own belly and gut, and its soul was as fleshy as a pair of buttocks stamped with a simplistic, arrogant slogan: 'I don't give a damn about anything that isn't me, about anything that isn't this oh so beautiful, palpable, desirable me, about anything that isn't pleasure and power.'

The little old woman with the spotted, half-tarnished mirror rescued from a rubbish skip offered a very different view of things. She spoke of the vulnerability of the flesh and its slow erosion by the march of time. But more than that, when a body was gradually being uprooted as hers was, one could look through its withered, worn-out, gently faltering exterior, and see that what lay inside had many different facets. Just as a dense ochre is made from a mixture of colours, so the body incorporates a variety of forms and forces which it is impossible to distinguish at first glance. You have to stare at the ochre for a long time and with great patience and attention before you can begin to make out the colours it is composed of; and it is easier to do that when the ochre is already faded and washed out by rain and sun. Then you can pick out the shades that have been used, and work out the order and quantity in which they have been mixed together. First you work back to a violet base which was turned brown with pure yellow. Then the violet separates into purple and blue, the quantity of which you need to work out. In the same way, if you observe a person for long enough, you can see through their external appearance and discover other figures inside them, and varying quantities of light and shade. It tends to be in very old people that the body shows most noticeably through to the surface. The fact that they no longer need to bother about their physical appearance gives them a certain happy-go-lucky attitude and an almost naïve openness in the expression of their feelings. But the same touch of early childhood shines through in plenty of other people as well: lovers, husbands, wives and parents, people doing laborious jobs or keeping vigil, people who suffer pain, fatigue, sorrow or illness, people in mourning. In some of them the inner elements conflict and harden into coarse black lumps, whereas in others the whole picture becomes a fluid play of light and limpidity. The little old woman with the mirror was one of those.

And in her case there was something more coming through to the surface than just a variety of bodily components. Other, even more translucent outlines could be glimpsed as well. There was a kind of halo emanating from her. It wasn't that she was beginning to give out a supernatural light, like a saint

74

in an icon; she wasn't like that at all, she was just a perfectly normal woman who had been relieved by old age of the burden of herself, and stripped of her most cumbersome conceits. That fragile halo was certainly not a nimbus of glory, it was simply her aura – what is known as the ethereal body, which is said to surround every physical body, but which no-one, or almost no-one, can see.

And here was he, Prokop Poupa, suddenly beginning to see this immaterial body, right here in the street, around a woman he did not know, when it was thirteen degrees below zero. His gaze touched that invisible body and brushed against it, and his own flesh, under his freezing cold skin, began to quiver with a tremendous new feeling of tenderness for the world and the people in it.

The old lady thanked him and trotted off, taking careful little steps among the patches of ice. And her frost-coloured aura trotted along around her. Prokop watched her go. It was only then that he noticed that she was wearing odd stockings; the one on the right leg was brown, and the one on the left lime green.

He went back to his rake and got down to work again. Sometimes he glanced curiously at a passer-by, but his eyes had already lost the strange sharpness of vision that had been bestowed on them for a moment.

No matter: there are visions which, however fleeting, leave indelible traces in the memory. Ever afterwards the mind prowls round them, and the heart waits close by. Waits and hopes, without even knowing what for.

4

Every year when spring came around Prokop was seized by a sudden urge to tidy up. At the first signs of fine weather and birdsong, off he went, throwing himself into yet another attack on the disorder which reigned in his home. But the results were usually less than satisfactory, since he tended to stir up far more mess than he removed.

That spring he decided to classify the many packs of photos that were lying around all over the place in his flat, so he got them together in a great heap on the kitchen table and started to sort them out. But straight away he found himself in a dilemma: by what criterion was he going to arrange them? Chronologically or by subject? And if by the latter, how was he to decide what the subjects should be? As for chronology, it could only be very approximate since Prokop had no memory for dates.

But the biggest problem was that some of the photos were books in themselves, which gave off rustles and murmurs. Many stories, and yet more things left unspoken, whispered to each other in these rectangles of matt or glossy paper; many labyrinthine complexities were coiled up under what was visible on their fine surface layers. And as Prokop looked down at these feather-light universes lying in the palm of his hand he would stop, his mind completely engrossed in the picture, his memory on full alert. He would use his eyes to listen out for sounds, and relying on his sense of smell more than his sense of touch, he would search around in the grain of the paper to rediscover the odour of the place and the skin of the people shown in the photo.

People's smell: that is the first thing that fades in the memory and weeps with pain at times of mourning and separation, the thing that can least endure the absence of the body that carried and emanated it. The smell of the hair, the neck, the forehead, the lips, the shoulders . . . Prokop breathed in the empty air.

The smell of Marie's body: for a long time it had continued to permeate Prokop's skin, springing back to life sometimes in his dreams with such force that it woke him up with a start and plunged him straight into a state of anguish. He had had to struggle to cast out of his flesh the illusion of her smell that still lingered in it, and strangle the wild yearning to recall this most intimate trace of his unfaithful wife. He had tried very hard, on the other hand, to conserve beyond death the odour of his mother's, then his sister's skin; these were subtle, very discreet perfumes, sweet and mild. But they had all faded to nothing in the end, then the voices had disappeared in their turn.

In the end Prokop selected three photos from his jumbled heap: one of Olbram at the age of eight, one of Olinka at fifteen, and one of the two children together when they were five and eleven, standing in front of a low stone wall in the country with a basket full of gooseberries at their feet, a dying twig fire beside the wall, and a big cloudy sky overhanging the scene. He set these three apart to give to his friend Jonás, so that he could make new prints of them, enlarged and retouched in his old-fashioned way.

He was still rummaging through his photos when the doorbell rang. It was Big Baba, gasping for breath after climbing five floors. Every spring she mustered the willpower to go up all those stairs and visit Prokop, whose lofty perch was full of the sounds of birds calling and singing down in the courtyard aviary, whereas she lived in a ground-floor apartment facing on to the street, and heard nothing from one season to the next but the noise of cars and trams.

As every year, Prokop sat his friend down in the armchair in his bedroom, next to the open window.

They never talked much during these visits, since Baba's main reason for coming was to converse with the birds. Looking out into the courtyard, she would improvise long, melodious consultations with the sparrows. It was a truly remarkable sight: this enormous woman, her features marked by age and fatigue, always dowdily dressed in some shapeless garment, making these crystal, whistling sounds. Her eyes misted over with a soft radiance, her rounded lips made her mouth seem tiny, and her whole body, normally reminiscent of a prehistoric deity, seemed to grow lighter as she moved her hands gracefully in time to the rhythm of her songs.

One day Prokop asked her what on earth she and the birds were talking about.

She answered, calmly and seriously: 'They tell me how hungry they are. Birds are always hungry, because every day they have to find enough food to equal the weight of their own bodies. And they also tell me how hard the long journeys are that they have to make to escape from our cold winters, and what a bitter struggle it is for them to get a place to live and keep it, how hard it is to find a mate, how much toil and perseverance it takes for them to feed their young who are born with hunger in their bellies, and finally that they live in constant fear because there are so many predators forever wanting to eat them and their little ones.'

'Is that all? They're just hungry and scared to death all the time?' asked Prokop.

'No, of course not. They also sing of the power and the glory of desire, the splendour of the places they fly over, the infinite vastness of the sky, the joy of light. They speak of the ardour of passion, their love of the earth and the sky, of the rocks, hedges and forests. They proclaim the fullness and intensity of life that urges them on. They shout for the joy of being the song of the earth and cry out to the four winds the glory of being birds.'

'All in all then,' Prokop remarked, 'they're the same as us. They have a bloody awful time from the minute they come out of their shells the way we do out of our mother's womb, they have to fight on every front and look out for themselves the whole time, but just like us they're proud of belonging to their race, and they put off as long as they possibly can the fateful moment when they have to die.'

'Yes and no. They at least never do evil for the sake of evil, they are what they are and act only in accordance with the strict laws of their nature. They have nothing to feel guilty about, unlike us. And so they're entitled to ask God for an explanation.'

'How's that?' marvelled Prokop, who at that time was still more amused than genuinely concerned by such talk.

'There are some really sweet things about birds in the Gospels, written on God's behalf,' Baba went on, 'that they don't need to worry about a thing, that God will see to all their needs. But the poor little creatures don't always share that opinion when they're sitting on a frost-covered branch dying of cold or hunger or thirst, or when they get torn to shreds by a cat, or ripped to pieces by a sparrowhawk, or perhaps get a bullet put through their hearts by some damn fool hunter. The good Lord's dear little birds rather feel that they've been conned, and that He's neglected them pretty badly.'

'I must say they tell you some tall tales, these renegade birds of yours! But what do you say to them in return, do you tell them that it's no fun being a human being either?'

'I don't tell them anything, what do they care about what happens to us? I ask them a question. Always the same one. One single question.'

'What is it?'

'It's a secret between the birds and me.'

'Fine, but do they answer you?'

'No, well, not exactly. I'm sure I don't sing well enough to make them really understand me. Who knows? But I keep on and on asking my question all the same. I ask the sparrows, blackbirds, crows, thrushes and tits, the swallows and larks and nightingales, and the rooks in winter as well, and the gulls and swans. I ask all of them.'

Prokop listened to Big Baba conversing with the birds; she was just having a chat with the cuckoos, judging by the piercing double notes she kept repeating over and over again. It created a very soft interplay of echoes between the window and the trees.

But the interplay of echoes went still further than that. It reverberated to and fro between Prokop and the birds, between all the living, between the earth and the heavens, between space and time. Between the living and God. Because by now Prokop understood what the question was that Big Baba kept asking over and over again. Everything that in the past, and even up until recently, had for him been no more than amusing word-play and verbal jugglery, would from now on, and more so every day, be a matter of deepest importance. He felt that henceforth what was at stake was his whole being and everyone else's as well, all at one go, at every moment. It was now becoming clear to him that all those household gods whom he and his friends had summoned up one evening at the Little White Bear had answered the call and taken up their stations exactly where they had been told to. And far from protecting his friends and himself from external dangers, they were instead flushing out the internal enemy that each one of them was hiding or even unwittingly fostering. Their guardian spirits had in fact infiltrated their inmost being. And now that the sly foe within was unmasked, and its crime exposed – how, seemingly all innocence, it had reduced their being to the grotesque proportions of an 'obscene body' – it really had no option but to come out into the open and admit in broad daylight just how mean and vile it was. At least that was how it was for Prokop; no doubt his friends were having rather different experiences, but he wasn't yet in a position to judge what they were going through. For the moment he was too fully preoccupied with his own strange inner upheavals, and far too hesitantly groping along in his own darkness to be able to venture into that of his friends and see clearly there. In the case of Big Baba however, he did suspect that the question she kept asking in her conversations with the birds must centre on God. On God's mercy. Or at least on His justice and the dubious goodness of His Creation. What did the birds have to say about it? The same as men said. That the world is beautiful and the light glorious, that desire is intoxicating, that life is full of pleasure. Well and good: but they also cried out that they were hungry and afraid. They told the truth that beauty can be bitter, that the desire that burns in other people's guts can be cruel, that life can be brutal. And above all they said how hard it is to conquer the pure space of light, how painful it is to gain access to splendour.

It was getting cooler outside, and in the end Big Baba closed the window. Her question remained hanging amid the new leaves sprouting on the trees. Prokop made some coffee which they drank in the kitchen while looking through the photos that were still lying in a heap on the table. There was one, now yellow and cracked, which held Prokop's attention. It was from more than fifteen years before; it had been taken in the country, on a day in autumn, in front of his mother's house. It showed five people, a dog, three hens, two geese and some apple trees. In the background you could see the house, partly hidden by the old apple trees which were heavy with fruit. There was a ladder leaning halfway up one of the trees, and on it was perched a man who was reaching out with his arms towards the branches. This was Prokop's brother-in-law Marek. The woman at the foot of the tree was smiling and standing in a rather ungainly posture with her arms held somewhat apart from her round-bellied body. This was Magda, his first wife, pregnant with Olinka. Side by side in the centre of the photo stood Prokop and his mother; he had one arm round her shoulders. In the left-hand corner in the foreground was Romana. Her full skirt was being lifted up to the left by the wind, as were the long twisted locks of her dishevelled, greying hair. From the way she was standing off to one side, teetering in the wind that was blowing in her skirt and hair, and also apparently balancing on one leg only because the other one was extended so far that the foot was out of the picture, it looked as if she was about to go off the edge of the photo at any moment. One of the hens was pecking quite close to her, another was over by an apple tree, while the third seemed to be sitting on her eggs in the grass at the foot of the ladder. The dog, a mongrel with long white hair called Mrácek, was sauntering along in front of the house with his bushy tail in the air, while the two geese, their necks stuck out at an angle, strutted about one behind the other between two apple trees.

An ordinary photo of an ordinary family on an ordinary day, and not very well centred. But it was precisely because it was less than perfect that it caught Prokop's eye after all this time. He was also intrigued to know who on earth could possibly have taken it. A neighbour or someone who had just dropped in for a brief visit? Prokop couldn't remember any more, and it didn't much matter.

The hens, the dog and the geese, had died long ago; his mother about ten years ago, his sister eight. His mother had died of cancer, his sister of a chill in the soul which had driven her one evening to go and lie down in the snow of an icy winter so that she would never have to get up again.

What age would Romana have been now? Prokop did a rapid calculation. She would have been fifty-seven. He took the photo and put it on one side with the picture of the children, so that he could take it to Jonás too and get him to make an enlargement just of Romana. Romana with one foot cut off, as if she were already being pulled up from the earth by the roots.

Perhaps Jonás, with his ability to make all kinds of astonishing metamorphoses and anamorphoses happen in the world of the visible, would be able to give Romana back her off-camera foot and provide a glimpse of the elsewhere towards which his sister was limping off.

5

When anyone turned up to see him at home, which was not often because he didn't like visits much, Jonás went straight into a state of manic restlessness. He jumped around all over the place, offered coffee, tea, wine, beer, biscuits, gherkins and salami all at the same time, opened the cupboards, refrigerator and drawers and stuck his head into them like a fox-terrier scenting a hare, re-emerged every time looking terribly shamefaced because they were all so pitifully bare, marked each new disappointment with a soft, singsong 'shit shit shit', then ended up giving his visitor a glass of water or milk and mumbling incoherent excuses.

Jonás ate practically nothing, and drank only water. He was a strange figure, small, very slender, with large bronze eyes which always seemed astonished and grew misty with melancholy for no reason at all. He lived on air, on the colour of the sky, on the wind and on his own dreams. He slept as little as he ate, going to bed very late so that he could work on his photography, and getting up very early to walk round and round the city before going to the factory where he had a job as a packer.

The moment Prokop got to his place, Jonás began his St Vitus' dance and launched an attack on his empty cupboards.

'Forget it,' Prokop said to him, 'there's never anything to eat in your hermit's cell. Come and tell me what you can do with these photos instead.'

Jonás jumped down from the chair he was perched on, looking very proud of himself because he had actually managed to unearth a packet of vanilla wafers and a few musty teabags. He put some water on to boil, then opened the envelope containing the four photos that Prokop had brought and took them out, while Prokop vaguely explained to him what he wanted.

The tea was quite disgusting. Prokop pulled a little flask of rum out of his jacket and emptied the contents into his cup, thus concocting a toddy with an indefinable taste of almonds, petrol fumes and dust. Once he had drunk it, he got up and went to have a quick look in the bathroom. All along the clothes lines that were fixed up over the bath hung rectangles of paper on which the same sombre landscape kept repeating itself like a melancholy refrain. Then he went into the room where Jonás kept his prints. Jonás rummaged around in boxes and cartons and handed Prokop a large pile of photographs. Prokop spread them out on the wooden floor and got down on all fours to browse at random through the scattered images.

There were still lives — potatoes, pears, bunches of grapes, sweet peppers . . . Jonás had photographed them just as they were: everyday fruit and vegetables sitting on a wooden table or on the floor, without any accessories or special lighting effects to embellish them. The whole of this series was in black and white, or more precisely in grey. Every shade of grey, from the darkest to the palest, was on display here; every fruit, every vegetable, was a solid mass of grey, a dense stone made of vegetable matter whose surface was alternately silky and rough. Fruits steeped in the silt of the earth and of the centuries, vegetables ripened deep underground from seeds sown by the long, long sleep of the dead. Thousands of years of sleep.

It was hard to tell if these fruits of the earth were meant for the living or the dead. Suffused with greyness and muted light, hewn from the very stuff of silence, clay, dust and rock, they seemed like pieces of dross thrown out by some volcano buried deep under the earth's crust. There were potatoes that looked like pumice stones and pears like bulging flints. The cauliflowers were reminiscent of grainy rocks puffed out with chalky crystals, the sweet peppers of solid steel castings. Yet Jonás had neither added anything to, nor subtracted anything from these simple products of the earth. He had looked at them for a long time, set them down on the wooden surface of his table or on the ledge of a window blurred by grime and rain or frost or condensation, then seized hold of his camera and captured the image that had imprinted itself on his mind. That was how he had seen it, not otherwise, and he was reproducing that vision.

There were no bouquets of flowers in his series of still lives: just one flower on its own. It was a peony that had lost half its petals, with a milk bottle for a vase. The bottle had not been washed; it had a creamy deposit around the bottom, and there was a milky blur inside it which made the glass opaque. This makeshift vase looked as if it was made of fine porcelain, or even translucent mother-of-pearl, and the few remaining petals at the top of the stem above the neck of the bottle were velvety white, as if the stem had absorbed all the milk and passed its richness and colour on to the delicate flower. As for the petals that had fallen, they were so light and opalescent that you could almost see them evaporating before your very eyes. It was the silkiest, smoothest flower imaginable, and its creaminess was accentuated by the spiralling folds of shadow all around it.

The peony as seen by Jonás did not so much give off a perfume as breathe out a breath: that of a vegetable soul, of a being which consents to lose its strength and beauty, which has renounced everything in order to live only in the grace of self-forgetfulness and self-sacrifice, in obscurity, silence and absence. It was the most humble and patient of flowers; and it was also a prayer.

After the still lives came landscapes, views of fields, country roads, river banks and marshes. Jonás' vision had gradually broadened in range, but it was just as unadorned as before, or perhaps even more disconcertingly so. What was particularly striking about these photos was the ever-increasing sense that their subject matter was disintegrating, that the landscapes were about to fade away and disappear into a corrosive fog. Whatever was portrayed, whether mineral or vegetable, was broken up into a soft, shimmering mass of minuscule points, of melting shadows and specks of light clinging here and there like sharp twinkling stars to the pervading misty twilight.

There were ponds bordered with ashy grasses and inky rushes and foliage, their lead-grey water scored by a few silvery ripples. There were banks overgrown with bushes like granite boulders, covered in pale mauve grass and planted with slender poplars as frail as feathers which cast their quivering shadows on to rivers the colour of pewter; abandoned railway lines stretching away to the horizon, their passage marked only by lines of telegraph poles with broken wires; paths in parks lined with statues covered by tarpaulins, forest trails whose blackish mud gleamed with puddles of rainwater, staircases in old houses at the bottom of which mythical beasts eroded by the weather kept guard as if in an endless dream. And up above all these evanescent landscapes were expanses of sky, sometimes dark, sometimes shot through with flashes of metallic turbulence. There were also skies touched with the colour of columbine, tarnished gold or old ivory, and sepia forests, amber rivers, russet clouds threaded with gilt, purplish meadows and snowy suns. And you could feel the air and the wind in these places, and smell their smell.

But it was more than that; the wind that blew very quietly over these melancholy expanses was one that rose from a hinterland, and the light glistening through these skies had hatched in an indeterminate elsewhere. There was a fine, barely visible mist which gently broke the link between beauty and matter, matter and form. All these places seemed like ghostly visions with tremulous contours and shifting foundations. Like the little old woman with the mirror encountered one frosty day: the immaterial becoming perceptible.

There were yet more landscapes and strange cities. At the moment Jonás was composing his own scenes by cutting out cardboard shapes which he arranged on metal plates or in front of backdrops made of glassy paper or sheets of aluminium or plastic. Prokop noticed a field of ancient standing stones. It was like a moonscape with coal-black upright slabs of various shapes and sizes protruding from it which looked like hooded worshippers, penitents shrouded in darkness, weeping women petrified in their sooty tears. And the cardboard against which these solitary, hieratic figures stood out was deep black and splashed with whitish, fleecy clouds, like the smoke from a huge fire raging in some faraway place.

There was also an overgrown castle courtyard. Its walls were so high that they seemed to be rising up towards an infinity beyond the limits of the photo. The ground was cracked, littered with rubble and streaked with dust and gravel. The walls were bare, as was the courtyard; there was not a statue or a column, or even a step. Each wall had an opening set into it, but there were no doors. Dark blocks of shadow were coming in through these low, squat gaps. Or were they perhaps going backwards? It was hard to tell.

What Prokop noticed was that Jonás' photos looked more and more like battlefields where light and darkness were engaged in merciless, silent, icy combat. In every picture the battle was at its height, but the outcome remained unknown; would the light succeed in pushing back, subduing and breaking up that opaque darkness, or would the darkness devour and engulf the light? Looking at the photos it was amazing and almost frightening to be plunged into the heart of the fray like this, suddenly confronted by the birth of the world: or perhaps by a moment of its apocalypse.

Patches of light clung to the pitted walls, and some piles of gravel strewn on the ground glittered here and there with white-gold iridescence.

What was behind those gaping doorways? A thick casting of solidified darkness, an abyss plunging down to Hell, the threshold of nothingness or the black hole where everything began? Would the darkness come crashing out on to the sparse, sputtering granules of pure light on the courtyard, and either crush them and reduce them in their turn to nothingness, or spangle and bedazzle itself with them? Or were the shards of light about to surge into the gaps and demolish the darkness within them?

Looking at this ruined palace courtyard made Prokop feel tiny, and once again the question of salvation burst in on him. Would he never again be able to squat on a floor without colliding with the problem of grace and perdition?

Aloïs recreated the world in miniature and somehow managed to turn what was apparently just a children's game into a setting for the most wonderful images. Jonás made infinity out of next to nothing – pieces of cardboard, collage, sheets of metal, the odd pinch of plaster dust. Both cases represented a flashing tangential point at which the infinitely small met the infinitely large: a crossroads between time and eternity where the obscene body suddenly shuddered as it found itself confronted by its own wretchedness, and above all felt the shock of its own mortality.

Once again there was no distinction between the real and the imaginary. Everyday normality was rearing up, or rather plummeting, to the outer limits of the unknown and the disquieting.

Powerful, spellbinding and tragic, the darkness held sway; sharp, searing and even more tragic, the light asserted its authority. If you succumbed to the delights of sinking deep into the heaving black swells of the former you would lose yourself. You would do so just as surely if you exposed yourself to the piercing glare of the latter. You had to choose one or the other, there was no third option, even though most people did their utmost to steer an evasive middle course between the two.

Prokop tried to stand up. At first he couldn't get off his

knees because his back was too sore. After a while he drew himself up, little by little and with great care.

All this time Jonás had sat to one side, huddled up and silent. He always sat like this when one of his friends was spreading out in broad daylight the images he had worked on long and hard, all on his own. He didn't move or say anything, he just watched the person who was staring at his photos. His eyes were lit up with the utmost attentiveness, but not because he was waiting to hear his visitor's judgement; he didn't much care whether his talent received recognition or not. All he was interested in was watching the other person's gaze, and trying to get right through to the point where it originated. What counted was that others should see what he himself had glimpsed beneath the surface of the world, that they should share his curiosity and little by little open the many layers of eyelids which limit our vision. He wanted them to turn around and go back far behind their own eyes, to the very source of their gaze, and then penetrate further still, to the light that bathed the first days of the Creation, to that miraculous clearing that opened up in the primordial darkness, and draw from it the great power and passion of wonder.

As he sat curled up in a corner like this, staring at his guest's face, his own gaze ran all over the room, saturating it with dreams. It rested on the floor and the dozens and dozens of images scattered all over it, and at the same time it floated in space between the four walls. Then the visitor felt the visible world gently swaying all around him, and a confused desire to become transparent welling up inside him.

Prokop went over to the trestle table cluttered with cardboard boxes, pieces of cut-up paper, bottles of ink, glue, paint, jars full of sand, little stones and bits of broken glass.

'Is this where it all happens?' he said, pointing at the chaotic mess on the table.

'Yes, this shambles is where I do my work. The better it goes here, the less I take photos outside. In fact I don't need to go out at all, except to sniff the air, see what the weather's like, and pick up some bits and pieces of scrap to use in the photos. Everything is beautiful, even a rusty nail. You can do anything, invent anything, or tell any story with bits of old rubbish like this. I have great fun, I go on journeys on my table. You can travel long distances, anywhere you like, with a few little bits of paper and some filings and shards of glass . . .'

'Are those your standing stones?' asked Prokop, pointing to some little pieces of cardboard daubed with black felt-tip.

'Yes, I'm exploring Celtic landscapes at the moment. I'm wandering all over the moors.'

At these words an image passed rapidly through Prokop's mind. He saw two silhouettes clinging on to each other, walking against the wind over the vast expanse of a desolate moor. Lear and his Fool; Aloïs and Jonás. But he couldn't make out which of the two was walking in front. One moment the Fool, as light as an armful of hay snatched from a haystack, was scurrying and stumbling along behind Lear, hanging on to flap of his coat, the next he was skipping merrily, and the deposed king, head down and back bent, was zigzagging along behind him, clutching his belt. The image flickered several times at high speed before Prokop's eyes.

A few last rays of light suddenly cast white streaks on to the table where the two men's hands rested among the collection of waste items. The streaks grew larger, dwindled, swelled out again, then remained still for a moment. They changed colour as well; their white metallic gleam grew dull, they turned a bluish colour and then a diaphanous mauve, and finally they disappeared altogether. Prokop's hazy thoughts fluctuated along with them, then turned to lead as the room grew dark at last. On the floor the landscapes were drifting off into their own twilight murmurs. Slowly they melted and faded away into the shadows all around. The wind of the megalithic moors blew right up against Prokop's heart.

6

The summer dragged for Prokop. Being on holiday for the first time without Olbram made him feel very low.

Autumn came. Prokop and his broom chased the dead leaves; he and his dustbins put the rubbish out in an orderly fashion along the pavement; he and his rheumatism warmed themselves up in the evenings at the Little White Bear, where the discussions centred more and more on the events that were unfolding in neighbouring countries. Prokop and his household god held more silent conversations than ever in the toilet about the mysteries of the visible and the invisible, and the question of salvation.

October went by. There were many orangey-pink clouds to the glory of Olinka, and also moons which filled the nights with thoughts of Olbram.

The photos that Jonás had retouched were hanging on the bedroom wall: timeless portraits, eaten into by reddish, ochre and pale yellow mists, through which you could see Olinka's brick-red lips, hazel eyes and long pale hair, and Olbram's cherry-red lips and mauve-blue eyes. A third frame hanging below the others contained the photo of the children standing in front of a low wall. The cloudy sky had a turbulent bronze and pale green glow which reflected on to the close-cut grass, while the grey of the wall was so translucent that it seemed to be made of glass. The two children were as milky white as the smoke rising from the twig fire that was dying at their feet. Only their mouths had colour; they were bright red, like the redcurrants in the basket. Olbram and Olinka floated like two bright-lipped phantoms under a sky clad in armour made of bronze and lime satin.

There was also the enlargement of Romana. It was a black and white print, in the style of the lunar standing stones and the abandoned palace courtyard.

The photo brought out Romana's distress so powerfully that it couldn't possibly be hung on a bedroom wall. Prokop slipped it between the pages of a book.

In addition to these portraits, Jonás gave him some other photos which he had looked at especially closely.

'I got the feeling you liked these,' Jonás said as he gave them to him. 'It means they'll get an airing instead of staying cooped up in my boxes. And the air and light will do them good, you'll see, because as time goes by they'll go yellow and blurred. I deliberately take photos that are already in the process of disappearing, then little by little they fade as the daylight wears away at them. We really ought to do the same, all of us: fade away, fade away . . .'

November came, and one by one its rainy days began to go by. One afternoon Prokop went to pick up Viktor from the boiler room where he worked. That same morning a cartload of coal had been delivered, and the cellar was filled with a mountain of lignite so high that you couldn't see in through the little basement window. Viktor's overalls, hair, hands and face were covered in coal dust. He checked that everything was in order, made a cursory attempt to get the dirt off his face and arms, changed clothes, then went off with Prokop to have a beer.

There was a heavy, brown fog in the sky, and another fog, even more glaucous and foul-smelling, in the bar. After two pints they left, and took the tram over to the Vyton district. Radka was waiting for them in her printing studio in the attic of an old house.

When they got to the top landing Viktor took out his bunch of keys. They went through the first room of the attic, which was pitch dark and cluttered with discarded furniture and bits of planking. They had to bend down so as not to bang their heads on the beams, which at least meant that they had to watch where they were walking. Viktor knocked on a wooden door so worm-eaten that the heavy iron lock on it seemed laughably superfluous. One thwack with a shoulder and it would have given way instantly. Radka came and opened the door to let them in. She was muffled up in a thick pullover, woolly hat and mittens, but the tips of her fingers were red, as was her nose. Inside the attic it was icy cold.

'The stove has packed up,' said Radka by way of a greeting.

Piles of printed sheets lay in neat rows on trestle tables. The whole place stank of glue. A guillotine sat on a crate, its blade raised ready for use. There were also two presses and a spirit roneo. Reams of paper were piled up on a long wooden bench. The floor was covered in an assortment of fraying, threadbare rugs. Bare light bulbs cast an acid light over the whole messy scene. Radka offered to make coffee. She poured some water from an earthenware pitcher into a battered saucepan and put it on to boil on a portable stove which was sitting on a camping table.

'There's no sugar left,' she warned. All the time she kept sniffing, non-stop; the cold was making her nose drip and each of her words came out in a little cloud of steam. Prokop and Viktor leafed through the completed pamphlets. All three of them talked about the demonstration that was due to take place that day.

'We'll see what happens,' said Radka, stirring the cups of coffee. 'In any case the procession is going to go right past here on its way down from Vysehrad, so we've got ringside seats. We'll go and join them.'

They got down to work. Soon all that could be heard in the icy attic was the rustling of paper, punctuated by Radka's sniffs and the muffled creaking of the beams. From time to time Radka stopped sorting pages and went to check whether the glue on the bindings was taking properly. Padding around in her slippers she made little disturbance.

A few posters and pictures were pinned on the walls, all of them crinkly and swollen with the damp. Among them were some warped, yellowing photos by Jonás, and also several portraits of writers and poets. Rimbaud rubbed shoulders with Anna Akhmatova and Jiří Orten. Hanging on a nail from a crossbeam was a brown-spotted mirror with a diagonal crack across it, in which you could see the reflection of a portrait of Bohuslav Reynek that was sellotaped to the side of a tall cupboard. The whole interplay of staining, warping, and inversion had the effect of accentuating the look of anxious, thoughtful melancholy on his face.

> *Smile just a little, despite everything . . .*
> *Otherwise I shall know that the mirror I see*
> *is held by a stranger*
> *and that it is myself that I am talking to,*
> *that it is me alone that I paint,*
> *I whose smile, in the depths of my heart,*
> *is chained up and beaten.*

In the reflected photo Reynek, so thin, so puny, and above all so humble, was sitting with his hands folded on his knees, next to an earthenware stove, with a cracked wall behind him, in the half-light of his house in Petrkov. There was no smile on his face with its high forehead and lowered eyes. But in the depths of his heart, perhaps, there was the faint gleam of a smile, tenuous yet enduring, like a grain of mica embedded in a dark rock. And at the depths of his sadness – most certainly – was the pure radiance of self-renunciation and of a very simple hope.

Radka was a bit like that as well, with her thin little face, always looking anxious as if she were perpetually trying to solve a riddle, and padding around noiselessly without disturbing the air around her. She laboured in the shadows, and her work was poetry. She didn't write any herself, or if she did, she kept it hidden. Maybe she just composed it in her head, shaping the verses out of silence. But it would have been hard for her to tell the difference between her own poems and the many others which she had read and reread until she knew them by heart: thousands and thousands of stanzas which she now carried around inside her. She was a vast living anthology, a sort of lyrical samizdat made of flesh, bone and nerves. In order to keep broadening her poetic horizons even further, she herself translated a great deal of poetry from a number of languages, even from Latin. Recently she had translated *Praises* by the abbess Hildegarde of Bingen. A work like that must have seemed utterly laughable to the police; they were much more likely to treat Radka's clandestine publications with contempt and indifference than to persecute her for them. Their henchmen must have thought it was crazy and totally ridiculous for someone to spend their free time getting frozen toes and hands in a dusty attic just in order to produce flimsy copies, printed in mauve ink, of nonsense like this:

> *Oh gentle chosen one,*
> *You who have shone forth in the ardour of the ardent,*
> *Oh root, in the splendour of the Father*
> *You have dispelled the mysteries . . .*

Rustles, creaks, sniffs. Prokop and Viktor continued their monotonous ballet round the tables, Radka zigzagged from the trestles to the benches, from the press to the guillotine. Three bags were already full of completed pamphlets.

Suddenly there was a great uproar. It was coming up from the street, and it was getting louder. Viktor, Prokop and Radka looked up and listened, unable to believe their ears. And yet there was no doubt about what they were hearing; a large, very calm, and very determined crowd was moving down the road at an even pace, chanting the word freedom. Radka perched on a stool to try and see what was going on through the dormer window. All she could make out was a throng of heads and a stream of candle flames. They rushed down to join the crowd. All the same Radka, so used to being cautious that by now it was automatic, took the time to turn off the light and lock the door behind her. On the other hand she forgot to put on her shoes, and so took part in the demonstration wearing apple-green slippers.

The procession slid down towards the river. The trams along the embankments, forced to slow down as the crowd grew bigger and bigger, were full of gawping faces pressed against the windows. Suddenly all those faces staring wide-eyed in the acid light of the carriages seemed unreal and anachronistic. The normal daily routine had just been turned on its head; all at once it was no longer time for everyone to take the tram and go home. The journey was coming to an unexpected halt at the halfway point.

In the end the passengers got out of the stationary trams and joined the procession as it turned round the corner at the National Theatre. On the steps of the theatre, framed from head to foot in the golden light from the picture windows, the usherettes in their black dresses stood as straight as little soldiers on parade and waved their hands as a sign of support.

But a little further on, in Narodní Avenue, policemen with truncheons in their hands were lying in wait for the demonstrators. Their attack failed, causing only a temporary panic. This month of November would answer to the joyful salutes of usherettes, not blows from truncheons. The whole city turned into a theatre, the whole country came on stage, and soon the castle opened its doors to a playwright. A new repertoire was on its way.

THE STEPS THAT DANCE IN
HELL

1

The wind of chance, wonder and encounters had brought
Prokop's heart to life. The wind of words and images had
worn away at it, slowly and insistently. And the wind of history had just turned the whole gloomy world around him
upside down.

The seed of slight madness inside him continued to germinate. During the long grey days it had sprouted thickly,
somehow managing to flourish on the slenderest resources,
drawing dew from every tear, light from every face and
nourishment from the tiniest speck of dust. And now here was
the flower breaking through, trembling in its early bud, yet
inevitably destined to open gently out.

Prokop was no longer a pariah. He could even have gone
right to the top. But once the euphoria and bustle of the first
few weeks following the revolution were over, he began to
beat a discreet retreat into his own inner world.

True, he wasn't a pariah any more; but he had lost his place
as a leading player.

Freedom, freedom! the crowd had shouted as they came
down one fine day in November from the heights of the
Vysehrad cemetery. Freedom – that's all very well, but to do
what exactly? After all Prokop's years of struggle and all the
torments and insults he had suffered in the name of freedom,
the battle to win it back was finally over. But already it was
making huge demands of a different kind. The whole enter-
prise was drifting off in a new direction, towards a far-off
horizon, one so remote that it seemed to belong to another
planet.

The magnificent name of freedom began to quiver and shed
its air of haughty superiority. It called out for self-sacrifice

and self-abnegation, in darkness and silence. It screeched in the song of the birds, howled in the wind, and shone through the haloes which sometimes radiated from people's faces.

At least the days of the broom and floorcloth were over. Prokop was offered a university post. He hesitated, and in the end turned it down. He no longer had the urge to teach; teachers had to talk with authority, and that wasn't his style any more. How could he trust himself to hold a discussion with a group of students when all he had done for years was soliloquise, either sitting in his own home or out sweeping steps? True, when he hadn't been holding forth to himself he'd been nattering in the pub, but that was hardly a main-stream educational activity either. It was not at all surprising that after twenty years of all this his ability to discourse was somewhat rough at the edges.

But now those evenings in the bar were a thing of the past as well; the meetings at the Little White Bear had stopped. Radomír had gone into journalism, Big Baba was a member of parliament, Viktor was playing in a jazz band, Radka had got a grant to study in Berlin, Aloïs was busy in the theatre, and Jonáš was preparing to move to the country where he could get on with his work in peace and quiet. It was the same with his other relatives and acquaintances. Everyone was on the move, both mentally and physically. Some were really moving on, accurately getting the measure of the changes that had taken place and exerting themselves accordingly. Others were too overcome by dizziness to do more than just wave their arms about wildly and blindly follow the misleading impulses of their heart and spirit.

Prague was like one of those large ornamental hourglasses filled with tiny grains of sand of various colours; when you turn it upside down all the grains take off and swirl about inside the glass ball, making fleeting arabesques and moving pictures. We marvel at this sudden eruption of new forms and rhythms, we follow its twists, turns and glittering undulations. We watch how, little by little, the farandole slows down, and how certain beads, delirious with lightness, keep gracefully twirling while others fall to the bottom more quickly and heavily and pile up in heaps which gradually become opaque. Then all movement ceases, and the layers of colour settle to create a new overall picture, different from the old one but not completely the reverse of it. We take note of this new order, and gradually get accustomed to the way the sand looks now that it's been reorganised. Then we put the hourglass back on the shelf, and life goes on.

Prokop opted for publishing, and went on to the editorial staff of a literary review. Given his awakening and indeed growing mistrust of language, he felt better equipped to deal with the written word than the spoken. When he was writing an article he could take the time to weigh up the meaning of his words and put his thoughts in order as clearly as possible. For many years he had allowed himself to be seduced by the sounds, resonances and reverberations of words, and had revelled in language like a bard inspired by the wind and the foaming waves, with 'a mouth ripe for the sorcerer's song/ telling the tale of his tribe/the enchanted rune of his race'. Now things had changed. He no longer felt words melting in his mouth and throat into great showers of speech. What he had in his throat instead was a gnawing anxiety, and there was an indefinable doubt running round and round in his heart. Barred from the game of runes and rhymes, he could feel a curious silence murmuring inside him, demanding more and more of his attention. He could no longer speak with a poet's voice, any more than with a teacher's, and he didn't want to either. He applied himself to pursuing the plain, pruned-down reflections to which any sucker off a main plant, whether beautiful or misshapen, is limited.

Visitors, too many for his liking, came to see him at the office. One afternoon the door opened and in came a young man with close-cropped hair, wearing faded jeans and a black shirt. Prokop said hello and waited for the stranger to introduce himself.

'Hey dad, don't you recognise me?' said the young man, smiling.

Prokop fell back in amazement on to his chair. It was Olinka. She came over and gave him a kiss.

All he could do was splutter: 'But – what have you done to your hair?'

'I've cut it!' was all she said in reply. She sat down on a corner of the desk and fished a packet of cigarettes out of her shirt pocket.

'Is it all right to smoke here?' she asked, then lit up without waiting for an answer.

Prokop couldn't speak; he just pushed the already full ash-tray over towards her. He was furious, but he could see that there was no point in arguing with her. She announced that she was planning to come and live in Prague. She had already enrolled at the Arts Faculty, she was going to study Spanish and Portuguese, and she would be sharing a flat with two girlfriends.

'You could have lived with me,' said Prokop.

'I'm not going to disrupt an old bear's habits,' she replied with a smile. She kept laughing all the time, lightly, brilliantly, and just a tiny bit idiotically, as people do when they are in love. It was clear to Prokop that she had not just embarked on her studies at university, but also on a love affair. It wasn't long moreover before he learned that the man for whom Olinka had a drunken heart and a shaven head was a third year medical student called Philip.

2

Another day, Prokop had a visitor who disconcerted him just as much as Olinka had with her new street urchin image. A big fat fellow came crashing into his office and walked over to him, muttering a brief hello. For a moment Prokop was nonplussed, then he realised who it was: his neighbour Mr Slavík, wearing the inevitable red scarf which by now was pretty much in tatters. Prokop, who hadn't come across him for so long that he had almost forgotten what he looked like, was quite taken aback by the sight of him in a new context, suddenly translated from the seedy dimness of the staircase to the brightly-lit surroundings of his office.

Without preamble Mr Slavík handed him a slim notebook.

'This is for you,' he mumbled in his deep bass voice, tugging at his long scarf of mourning, now faded from red to orange. 'Read it when you have the time.'

Prokop took the manuscript and asked: 'What's it about, Mr Slavík? Please, do sit down.'

'No, no, I don't want to disturb you. I was just passing. Anyway, if you read the story you'll find out what it's about. Goodbye, and thanks.'

He turned straight round and headed for the door. Prokop tried to make him stay, but it was to no avail, so he sat down again and leafed through the exercise book. Slim though it was, it wasn't even full. Only about ten pages were covered in large, very neat handwriting. It was a short story, with the uninspiring title 'Untitled'. On the inside of the cover the author had written a dedication: 'To my Dog'.

'Well well,' thought Prokop as he gazed at his taciturn neighbour's schoolboy handwriting, 'so Slavík has got bitten by the writing bug, and all for love of his mutt!' He got down to reading the manuscript straight away.

To my Dog

UNTITLED

One night in the middle of winter, when it was minus thirty degrees, I was born in a little village in the Krkonose. It was in February 1925. All over the sky there were stars as soft and white as drops of milk – it looked as though they were frozen too, my mother told me. She also claimed that you could hear wolves howling in the distance. My mother never lied. Apart from my dog and my mother, I have never known anyone who never lied.

I have nothing to tell about my childhood years in the village. Nothing happened except the simple events linked with the seasons, and my mother's baking followed the same yearly cycle. In winter we had maçaroons and cheese turn-overs filled with raisins, and at Christmas there were plaited almond cakes and sweets of different shapes and gingerbread biscuits. At Easter there were jam tarts and chocolate goodies, then bilberry, raspberry or blackberry cakes in summer, and apple and nut strudels in autumn. My mother never cheated, not even with the seasons. Just like my dog.

That's all there is to say about when I was a small child. I don't remember much except the food – and the way things smelt: the smell of the earth and the animals.

My mother didn't cheat with death either. She had never been ill. One day she went and lay down with a headache. Ten days later she was being buried. Afterwards we were told that she had had a brain tumour. It was like a mushroom that had grown under her skull: a big, greedy, out-of-control mush-room. When she went and lay down she knew straight away that she wouldn't be getting up again. People who spend their lives on their feet and are always busy never mistake the signs. For them, life is being in motion, and stopping is death. She always understood everything, my mother, like my dog. She didn't complain.

She was taken to the cemetery on a fine October morning. It was dry and cold, and the sun was shining very high up in a clear sky, like the copper pendulum of our clock which my mother polished until it gleamed. The road was lined with russet beech trees, and the paths in the cemetery were sprin-kled with a fine dusting of dead leaves whose soft yellow colour shone gold in the sun. I remember seeing that pale gold trembling in my tears. I was eleven.

That same evening my father got drunk, and from then on he never stopped drinking. He sold the house, left the village, and took me with him to Prague. We'd only just settled in, in the Zizkov district, when the Germans entered the city. I had just had my fourteenth birthday. My father, who until then had got sad when he drank, started to get violent. He was gradu-ally turning into a walking liquor-still, and as he did so his character got uglier and uglier. Sometimes he brought women

104

home. Since he beat them and insulted them, they didn't come back. So he went out and found more.

It was a time of violent death. People were dying from bullets and bombs, some on the battlefields, others in the camps from hunger and beatings. My father died right in the middle of the occupation – not as a hero or a martyr, but from drink. He fell under a tram with as much alcohol in his veins as blood: just a sour old wineskin bursting open under the wheels. Now I was on my own. I was seventeen. I left school and went to work in a factory.

The Germans were driven out of the country, but they were soon replaced by another army of occupation, so nothing much changed. At twenty-seven I married. Nine years later my wife left me for an accordionist from Mladá Boleslav who had a glass eye.

'OK, so he's missing an eye,' said my wife as she was leaving me, 'but he plays like a god!'

Given that she had never shown the slightest interest in music, I concluded that the divine qualities of her one-eyed man must be located in the lower regions of his anatomy. I've never been very keen on that side of things myself. So to cut a long story short, I was left on my own staring into space with two eyes that couldn't compete with the charm of one glass one. I got used to it very well. I never married again, or learned to play music.

Even so the evenings did seem long sometimes, so I hung about quite a lot in cafés. I played cards, but my heart was never really in it. In fact I got bored pretty quickly, wherever I was, whatever I did. I changed jobs quite a few times. I was a lorry driver, a post office worker, a removal man, a mechanic, a stretcher-bearer, a meter reader and even a cemetery attendant. From all of that I gained a huge amount of insight into people's behaviour. At the end of the day, although they seem different they're really all the same, brave and cowardly at the same time, stingy yet capable of making fine gestures now and again, wise or crazy according to circumstances, sometimes loyal and sometimes treacherous. But sublime, never, or at least very rarely! All that most humans do is trail around with them a crumpled, dirty, moth-eaten little soul at the bottom of their pockets — worse than that, a lot of them have holes in their pockets and so they mislay their ragged little souls as they go along without even noticing they've gone.

Then one day a dog came into my life. And that was when the boredom went out of it. It was just after the country was invaded in the summer of '68. He appeared from round a corner, on to a street that had tanks rolling along it. He was very young: a little mongrel with no collar, a bit short in the leg, with a powerful body, a bushy tail, ears like huge nettle-tree leaves, a long muzzle, and hazel eyes that glinted with orange lights. He had a beautiful coppery-red coat with a white bib.

He gazed up at me as if he was thinking something over, then followed me, wagging his tail. If I stopped, he stopped too, always keeping a distance of about two metres. His head was slightly bent and he kept giving me sideways looks. His eyes were good, full of wisdom and patience. Like my mother's. He went with me as far as my apartment block. When I went into the hallway, he made a show of going on his way. I went up to my flat and forgot about him. But the next morning, when I opened my door, I found him lying on the doorstep. He looked up at me and smiled.

That's how life is. Dogs do smile sometimes. And so I let him into the flat. He stayed there for eighteen years. The reason why he put off dying for so long was that he wanted to delay the moment of separation as much as possible. He knew very well that it would cause me pain. It has, far more even than he imagined.

The day he got into my flat after smiling at me, he inspected the two rooms and the kitchen, and set his heart on a narrow sofa sitting under a window in the living-room. He jumped on to it and looked at me, as if to ask if it was all right for him to be there. I nodded. And the sofa became his bed. I moved three times after that, and the dog and his sofa were always first into my new home.

I didn't try to find a special name for this animal, I just called him after what he was: Dog. Mongrel or not, he belonged to the canine species. As for me, I would have loved to be called Man – Mr Man, plain and simple.

Right from the start Dog and I got on like a house on fire. He was a quiet, solitary type. He was no more interested in seeking out the company of his fellow creatures than I was, and he trusted female dogs as little as I trusted women.

I began to read. At over forty years old I discovered books and the joy of reading. The great navigators who set off to explore the world and discovered new continents can't have been more astonished than I was when I threw myself into this new adventure. At the beginning I read just about anything. I went into libraries and took books out in alphabetical order. After a while I found my bearings, dropped the alphabetical system and used my intuition instead. One day I happened upon an author who completely knocked me for six. It was Strindberg. I'm sure I didn't understand much of it, but it really shook me. In fact that man affected me so deeply that I decided to learn Swedish. I studied it on my own. In the evenings at home I spoke Swedish to Dog, or rather I tried to speak it; I don't have much of a gift for languages. Dog lay on the sofa and listened attentively. I really believe that Dog could understand any language, because when he heard the human voice he listened only to the inflections of the heart.

Every morning and evening Dog and I went out for a walk. In the mornings I was the one who decided where we would go, and since I didn't have much time the route hardly ever varied; we just took a stroll around the area. In the evenings it was Dog who took me for a walk. He trotted along confidently and led me wherever he thought proper. I don't just mean that in a manner of speaking. He would lead me through street after street until we reached a square or a park which was really a proper place to go for a walk. There he would slow down, sniff the air and the earth, the roots and the grass, and the clouds as well. And I did the same. I wasn't as good at it as he was, but even so I breathed in diligently, and smelt the smell of the wind, the time and the light. With Dog I learnt how to smell, I learnt that everything has an odour, even sounds, colours, and passing time. I also learnt to look and listen in a different way. I began to perceive the world and people with the senses of a dog. In the end I loved life with a dog's heart. A heart that's always vigilant, but never anxious. A heart with a sense of smell and a passion for open space.

It was within myself that I found that open space, and it was Dog who helped me discover it. He taught me so well to keep my heart on the look-out that I scented an odour of infinity inside my own being. By taking me for walks through the city's streets and parks, Dog actually led me through the infinity of my inner self. And on the way I detected some tracks: ones left by God, or to be more precise, by his absence. I listened to his silence in me, watched his absence in me, and touched his emptiness. Some days I could feel with my finger-tips the peculiar consistency of his emptiness. I never prayed or went to church. I just walked through this desert of God. That's the way I, a man-dog, say my prayers.

I want to talk more about my dog's smile, even though it's impossible to describe. Dog had the smile of those who see right through the world and time, who feel with all their senses that real life is not fully present except at times when the silence of infinity flutters against the surface of the present moment, when the mystery of the invisible world comes and knocks gently against the simplest things – the wood of a table sticky with beer froth, the glaze of an earthenware mug, the banisters on a staircase, the crust on a cob loaf, a dustbin cover, a wall, a tree . . .

There were days when all at once Dog, for no apparent reason, would look up, prick his ears and listen. He had sensed an invisible presence which I could not feel, but which I then became aware of through him.

Dog had the smile of the chosen ones on whom the Angel has laid his hand. It was something I gradually came to realise as the years went by – that Dog was in fact the companion of the Angels. You may think that's raving nonsense or blasphemy, but it's not, and I'm not joking either. It's the truth. Maybe there are times when there is such a shortage of men worthy of being touched by the Angels that the Angels get discouraged and turn to animals. The fact remains that of the two of us, Dog and me, he was the one who was master. He was on a par with the Angels, he had the fire of their caresses in his coat and the softness of their light in his smile. I walked behind him, in his shadow.

I have already said that most human beings are pretty mediocre and uninteresting, and worst of all that many of them are very slovenly in the way they treat the poor little soul they have been given. They tear it to shreds and turn it into a cleaning-rag. Dog was different. He didn't have a soul, he was a soul. The gentlest and most modest of the great souls. An angelic soul with four legs and tawny fur. Sublime in his humility.

Dog got old. Little by little he grew deaf and blind, and then his hindquarters became paralysed. He spent almost all his time sleeping heavily and groaning. He was in pain. The vets I went to suggested putting him down, and some of the tenants in the building I lived in volunteered the same kindly advice. No-one had any idea what Dog was really like. What's more, if I had told them they would have laughed. They would have pointed out to me in their infinite wisdom that a dog of an angelic nature, even supposing that such a creature could exist, should never have grown so pitifully old, ugly and fat, let alone gone crippled and smelly. As if being touched by the light of the Angels meant that he was bound to be transfigured, forever beautiful and immune from the laws of biology. The laws of the body and time are merciless. My dog went through all the misery of old age, like any other living being. He wasn't spared. And why should he have been? By what right? Saintliness doesn't grant itself special privileges, far from it. It submits itself to the laws and duties common to all. But because people are so easily swayed by outward appearances and so slow to believe in anything to do with the heart, because their imaginations are stunted and hemmed in by preconceived ideas, they demand miracles before they will consent to believe in what they do not understand. Mystery can do without external miracles; the invisible world has no use for extraordinary phenomena. The supernatural is perfectly quiet and unobtrusive. And anyway, if God came down to earth and took human form as the son of simple people, if he suffered the torment and shame of a common criminal's death, why shouldn't an angel come in the form of a dog, a plucky, honest mongrel wandering in the streets of a city invaded by tanks?

Dog came to me, he never left me, he led me through infinite spaces that I didn't know existed and that no-one had shown me before. Dog was my guardian angel, my companion, my master. He was the light of my life. How could I have cut short that animal's life? I took care of him and watched over him. It was the very least I owed him.

Dog died. He went on ahead to scout out the territory. I still have his smile, it's always around me somewhere, and the softness of his fur is imprinted on the skin of my palms. I also still have a very little of his sense of smell deep in my heart.

It is with that heart that I await death. I'm not afraid. When it comes to take me, it will have the same walk and smile that Dog had in the days when he would come up to me as I got home from work and show that he wanted us to go out for a walk. Death will take me wherever it thinks proper, and that will be fine. I'm sure eternity has a smell too: a taste of pure light.

Mr Slavík's story stopped there, in mid-page. But on the following page he had written a few more lines. These were addressed directly to Prokop.

'Mr Poupa, I have not brought this piece of writing to you in the hope of having it published in a literary magazine. I'm not a writer. I've never written anything before and I won't be writing anything else again. I am entrusting this notebook to you because you are the only person I know who can read it in the right way. Don't misunderstand me, I'm not turning to you because you're a professor or a literary critic, but because you're a man in whom I think I have sensed the ability to be thoughtful and open to certain mysteries. As I've told you, my dog has left me a little of his ability to sniff things out, and I have a feeling that you are someone else who is "not alone". We're all "not alone", but sadly not many of us are aware of it. I believe I am right in thinking that you have been granted the same good fortune as I, although I don't know in what form.

'To be perfectly frank, I also think that you are as unworthy as I am to have received such a gift from heaven. Because let's not kid ourselves, neither of us is worth a great deal, and we're not going to end up having turned our lives into masterpieces, or even minor works of art. They'll be makeshift repair jobs at the very most. I'm sure you won't take exception to what I say, since you must have been willing to admit the same thing to yourself for a long time. I hope so anyway, for your sake.

'So that is why I'm telling you the secret about my dog. You will understand that it would be extremely embarrassing for me if this account were to be published, since most readers would be bound to find it ridiculous. I am counting on your understanding and discretion.

R. Slavík

Prokop leafed through the remaining pages; they were empty. He closed the notebook. He didn't know what to think of this piece of writing. Had he not known Mr Slavík, he would have read the story as a work of fiction, and dismissed the author's request for his writing to be kept in the dark as an amateur writer's coy attempt to get himself noticed by pretending to be an oddity. But Slavík really didn't seem to be the sort of man who would do something so conceited and ostentatious. And thinking back to the way he had reacted initially when he had read the title and dedication, Prokop now realised that he had been wrong there too. He no longer felt that his neighbour, like so many others, had been contaminated by the virus of writing, nor that Mr Slavík had called his story 'Untitled' for lack of inspiration. Nor did he consider this text to be the ludicrous product of an over-vivid imagination. Mr Slavík wasn't a crazed visionary any more than he was a pretentious scribbler. He was a simple man whose manner was gruff and whose behaviour was discreet and modest. He had written only to relate facts which he judged to be real, and had made no attempt to embellish them or to pepper them with extravagant anecdotes. Moreover he had given only very few details and had not even tried to prove that what he said was true. But that didn't mean that it wasn't. If Big Baba could converse with the birds, there was no reason why Mr Slavík shouldn't have talked to his dog in bad Swedish.

That evening when he got home, Prokop went up to the sixth floor and rang at Mr Slavík's door. It was opened by a stranger with a large black moustache, who told Prokop that the previous tenant had moved out almost a year ago, and that he didn't know where he lived now. Prokop then asked other tenants, but no-one could tell him anything. Mr Slavík had left without saying any goodbyes or leaving his new address with anyone. So Prokop waited for him to turn up and collect his manuscript. As the days went by, Prokop grew more and more impatient to see the man with the sense of smell and the heart of a dog who had honoured him with his confidence, albeit without showing much sensitivity for his feelings. The story this strange fellow had written was cranky, apparently nonsensical even, but it stirred up a great many questions in Prokop. Rather late in the day he sensed that his former neighbour was more than a brother in spiritual imbecility; he was a twin. A young brother in the darkness, as it were.

Mr Slavík never came back, and made no contact with Prokop. The man-dog didn't care what happened to his story and was not even concerned to know what effect it might have had on its one and only reader. Somewhere in the city or elsewhere he must have been carrying on his long solitary walk through his own inner desert. Prokop remained completely disorientated in his.

3

It was in the year following the revolution that Aloïs Pípal took his own life. Right from the beginning he had taken part in the demonstrations; the unexpected fervour that was rousing people and towns all over the country had swept him along and given him new vigour. Prague was in festive mood. The people in the streets looked different. Their facial expressions and even the way they walked were looser and more relaxed. The masks were discarded, fear had gone at last. Real life was back, bringing with it a particular sense of gaiety because it was being improvised from one day to the next, out in the street, like a travelling show. Life was climbing up on stage and enacting itself in a live performance.

As Prague celebrated, the whole city turned into a theatre, and in the midst of all the excitement Aloïs the actor, all bedazzled with dreams and hopes, made his entrance. His head was overflowing with plans, his heart with desires. He thought that the moment had finally come to make up for lost time and turn his dreams into reality: the ultimate reality, which for him was acting.

But as the months went by a sense of disquiet took hold of him. The pervading fervour of the early days was gradually subsiding, and already a new order of things was emerging and new structures were being set up – in which Aloïs wasn't managing to find himself a niche. More and more he felt that he was being left behind, gasping for breath and trailing along at the back of the race. The whirlwind that had caught him up was throwing him back out into the cold. Another life was beckoning, but he didn't seem able to reach out and grasp it. And he couldn't understand why.

It wasn't as if the theatre had closed its doors to him, in fact they were wide open again. There was nothing to stop him coming up from under the trap-door where he had been shut away for twenty years and re-emerging on stage. But he remained buried away in his hidey-hole. The fear in him was in a different place now; it had fallen into the depths of his heart.

No, he would never be able to play King Lear; another king had destroyed him, one called Ubu. He had rotted for too long in the cynic king's dungeon, and he couldn't find the way out any more. He hadn't the strength to heave himself up on stage, to take on a role, to become someone else and face the audience. The stage threw him into a panic, the audience even more so. It was not stage fright, it was a deep-seated malaise which affected his whole being.

Aloïs was no longer an actor, he was just an old wayside artiste whose spirit was broken, whose dreams were shattered and whose mind was deathly pale. Life wasn't a theatre any more, the stage was drifting away from him, driven on a raft out towards the open sea. And on that raft, all the words, gestures, laughs and cries were in the throes of dying. The play was over.

He put up a good show in front of his friends, and even managed to seem cheerful. But fear went on digging away deep inside him; he was losing his foothold in the land of the living. He developed a sense of humour that grew more and more flippant, and was sometimes quite disconcerting. He kept on discussing his plans, kept working. But he no longer believed in any of it. And one day he realised that he would never get over this fear that lurked within him, this indefinable feeling that he was going under.

> *My wits begin to turn.*
> *Come on, my boy. How dost my boy? Art cold?*
> *I am cold myself. (. . .)*

He was so cold that he no longer knew for sure which he was, the king or the fool.

'Poor fool and knave, I have one part in my heart/That's sorry yet for thee.'

He didn't recite any more, even in his sleep. He spent long sleepless nights with his eyelids closed, not moving. Lear's speeches passed in soft whispers through his mind, which was as bleak as a pale, flat desert.

'Poor fool and knave (. . .)'

He was sad about himself, about everything and for every-one. It was a sadness that could no longer be borne.

'He that has and a little tiny wit,
With heigh–ho, the wind and the rain . . .'

In the wind, heigh–ho, the dismal wind of fear from which there was no relief and no escape, Aloïs hanged himself, one October afternoon, in the cellar of his apartment block.

There was neither wind nor rain at his funeral, but bright sunshine and a large crowd. His friends were all there. They were in dismay; they didn't understand, or perhaps they didn't dare to understand. There was also a group of teenagers, come to salute the old stationmaster magician who had so often invited them to see his living-room railway. It was a salute to the enchantment of their childhood, now gone for ever. One of them was Olinka. She, like all the others, threw a rail ticket into the grave. Then she threw in another one, on behalf of Olbram. Aloïs' friends, seeing their children scattering tickets on to the coffin, suddenly felt so old they wanted to cry.

Olbram came to spend Christmas with his father. Sometimes he mixed English words in with his Czech. He liked his life in Peterborough. He wanted to be either a sailor or a conjurer, he hadn't yet made his mind up which. He already knew lots of conjuring tricks which he showed off to his father. He spent all his time making every small object he came across disappear. When he left, Prokop found that he had taken something away from him that he couldn't put his finger on: something in his way of seeing things, the city and other people. Sometimes Prokop was taken over by strange visions, all of a sudden, while he was fully awake. It was as if Olbram had distorted the crystalline lenses of his eyes.

It wasn't the same as on that winter morning when he had seen the aura shimmering around the old woman, nor was it like the feeling that he had had when looking at Jonás' photos, that he was glimpsing the invisible. Now it was dream bursting into reality, and sometimes even crashing through in a violent torrent.

So it was one day when, as he was standing ready to cross a street, he saw a little boy leaning on his elbows at a second-floor window of the house opposite. The child was blowing bubbles. Clusters of bubbles of all sizes were spurting out, scattering, bursting in flight or zigzagging very gently down through the air. One of these globules, all iridescent with mauve and green, streaked with golden strands and ringed with brilliant purple, came and floated right in front of Prokop's eyes. He just had time to catch a brief glimpse of his own upside-down reflection on the shimmering surface of the sphere, when plop, the bubble burst on the end of his nose. It was an odd little incident of no great importance, except that, for a few moments that seemed to go on for ever, it left Prokop with the feeling that his head was upside-down, and what's more that it was never going to right itself, and was now half-way up the walls and flying away down the street. He couldn't move forwards or backwards; suddenly, instead of seeing the world from the viewpoint of a biped firmly rooted to the ground, he was seeing it through the eyes of an opossum, hanging head down and weightless. Everything looked strange to him, he couldn't find his bearings or move a muscle in any direction, and he felt dizzy. His great bubble of a head, its eyes full of reflections of distorted images, wafted to and fro as far as the end of the street and eventually burst against a lamppost. Prokop felt the explosion reverberate through his whole being; his head returned to its right and proper position on his neck, he grabbed hold of it with both hands to make sure it was still there, then he blinked and tottered unsteadily off again.

In the spring Olinka moved with Philip into a one-room flat near Braník station. She had grown her hair again, but in accordance with the latest fad it was now wildly unkempt and dyed jet black. The flat was an artist's studio, lent to them by a friend who had gone abroad. Half the walls were glass from floor to ceiling, so although the young people had only a bare minimum of furniture, they had a great deal of light to make up for it. Inspired by this greenhouse brightness, Olinka

116

gradually filled the place with plants and cacti which she looked after with extreme care. Prokop suggested to his daughter that it might be a good idea if she showed the same concern for her hair; he couldn't get used to the systematic atrocities she kept inflicting on it. But Olinka paid no attention.

'You don't communicate with your own hair,' she explained to her father, 'whereas with plants you do. They have their own tastes, moods and feelings.'

So entirely convinced of this was she that she talked to them; and to make the dialogue more intimate she used her special language, Portuguese, just as big Slavík had chatted in broken Swedish to his angelic dog. Prokop began to love the plants, and always felt a certain inner turmoil when he looked at dogs and other animals. The man–dog's story continued to intrigue him, and the vegetal affections of his daughter waxed green and gentle in his mind.

4

One Sunday towards the end of summer, Prokop suddenly felt the urge to go back and see the statues by Mathias Bernard Braun in Kuks. Olinka and Philip went with him. They took the bus, and after a long voyage into the back of beyond they arrived in front of the old hospice, where the terrace bristles with statues whose names alone resonate with deep emotion and solemnity: Joy, the Angels of happy Death and pitiful Death, Religion, the Virtues and the Vices. Prokop stopped for a long time in front of the one representing Modesty, an allegorical woman whose softly swaying hips don't seem to fit with her veiled face. The veil falls right down to the hollow between her breasts, which swell, heavy and beautiful, beneath her stone dress, whilst the smooth curve of her stomach is emphasised by the folds of a cloak slipping half off her shoulders and wound around her hips. Her face only just shows through the veil and its vague outlines suggest that it could just as easily belong to an animal as to a human being.

It was this face which held Prokop's attention. Concealed for ever from the gaze of the onlooker under the dark grey veil of stone clinging to it like skin, it appeared to have no connection with the desirable body which seemed almost palpable through the porosity of the stone. In reality the languid body was melting in the dark fire of the flame of modesty that burned beneath the veil.

Wisdom on the other hand has three faces. There is one on the back of its head as well as the maliciously smiling one at the front, which in turn is reflected in an oval mirror. As for Hope, she is throwing her head back and gazing up at the light and the clouds in the sky, with one hand placed on her heart and her whole body trembling amid the swirling waves of her robe, which leaves one breast bare.

The Angel of pitiful Death follows on from happy Death to open the ball of the Vices, a series of figures which contort their greedy, tormented bodies as they grimace and stare into the void with crazed, furious or treacherous eyes.

The last time that Prokop had come to Kuks was one winter's day with Marie, at the beginning of their relationship. That day every gaze expressed nothing but the ardour of desire. The Vices and Virtues, which were even harder to tell apart than usual because their gestures and faces were shrouded in snow, ran the whole gamut of desire in all its variations – even Modesty, whose mask was perhaps just there to cover the ultimate expression of pleasure.

But, just as the Virtues and Vices go in a strictly ordered line from east to west, so too the love of Prokop and Marie had waned. From the tenderest dawn to a bitter sunset, with a fierce midday sun in the middle. From the bliss of passion to the pitiful betrayal of love. From the exultation of the flesh to flesh soured with tears.

They left the hospice terrace to go to the nearby forest of Bethlehem where Braun had sculpted great scenes from legends and the Gospels into the rocks. There the pair of hermit giants Garin and Onufrius call out to one another with their emaciated bodies, their crouching posture and their faces smothered by the swell of their beards and hair. They echo through the wood their insatiable hunger for openness and justice, their thirst for eternity, their holy terror and their undying love of God.

Saint Mary Magdalene lies at the edge of the path on a stone pallet, at the foot of silver birches which scatter her body with their leaves. She turns her face to look beyond the trees' foliage. There is nothing in her of the hermits' wild fervour. She is lying very peacefully, given over to the infinite sweetness of a love free of all fear and sorrow. Down there on the rock she dreams, without a care for the centuries which eat away at her body, for the rain and frost which corrode her tender mineral flesh, or the animals and creepy-crawlies which run over her robe. And yet her face is already half worn away; the fingers of the hand in whose hollow she has laid her head point towards a profile from which one eye has disappeared. She doesn't care; she can see now with the whole of her body, from which her heart and soul rise to the surface in an imperceptible puff of air. And the more her flesh disintegrates and disappears under a cover of moss and lichen, the more her joy shines through. The shape of her face is becoming blurred, but her smile remains, indestructible. Little by little her whole body is transforming itself into a smile, and even on the day when nothing remains of her but a stone returned to shapelessness, half buried under the earth and overrun by ferns, that stone will continue to radiate its brightness.

Prokop bent over towards the Penitent with her leper's face and smile of bliss. A little rainwater, coiled up in the folds of her robe, gleamed. A spider was spinning its web between her knees. A ladybird was climbing along her bare shoulder. An oak leaf quivered on her forehead, and the shade of the silver birches cradled the light that was shed on her body. Prokop sat down at her bedside and gazed at her smile. Modesty could not have had a more beautiful face under her veil than this Penitent who had put her past sins behind her and now thought only of the wonder of the new love which consumed her. Saint Mary Magdalene lay at Prokop's feet, and invited him to meditate on the mystery of forgiveness.

But suddenly Prokop's thoughts took off in another direction. Seeing this woman lying on the ground in the middle of the forest, he remembered Romana. This was the way she had been found, lying frozen stiff on the ground in the Divoká Sarka wood. But there was no smile lighting up her face. Her dress was soiled with soup stains, her face with tears. She had died in the desert of love, with no-one to console her.

It was about ten years now since this drama had taken place. But the further away the dead go in time, the more brutal the impact is when they suddenly rush back and knock on the memory of the living with their misty fingers.

It was not happy Death which had carried off Romana; and it was not so much a pitiful Death as a sorrowful one.

One evening as she was preparing Marek's favourite potato soup, she suddenly realised, with a certainty that struck her like a thunderbolt, that her husband was never coming back, and that by now his love for her was nothing but ashes scattered in the wind of forgetfulness and indifference. It was already several months since he had left her, but something in her had stubbornly gone on hoping and believing that her prodigal husband would return. She had swallowed her tears, shame and grief, and had waited. Despite the pain she was suffering, her love for Marek remained as strong and tender as it had always been, and she couldn't believe that he would stay far from this bright space for long. Very soon, she was sure, he would find his way back to the light. Were they not joined to one another by their vows, for ever? She had believed that. And now all of a sudden the illusion was coming to pieces. She had fallen into the trap of outdated romanticism, it had been very simple-minded of her really, and the self-deception couldn't hold up any longer. And her long wait crumbled to nothing, just like that, without warning, in front of the stove on which her smooth, creamy soup was simmering, smelling so deliciously of garlic and onion browned in butter, and cumin. Yes, it was quite clear that it was all over, she could just go to hell, she and her soup, she and her old vestal virgin's shrine of holy love. Marek was with another woman, he had thrown his wife on the scrap-heap and cared no more for her than if she had been an old-fashioned pair of worn-out shoes.

Suddenly she felt like a very small child, abandoned in the middle of a wasteground, far from anywhere. In her distress she didn't take time to think; her reason was blotted out by grief. She picked up the steaming soup pan, and without even turning out the gas flame or switching off the light, she went out. She opened the door on to the landing with one hand, and went downstairs with the pan held in the other, resting on her hip. She was wearing nothing but a grey and turquoise striped dress. Her legs were bare, and she had black ballet shoes on her feet. Outside the cold gripped her. The temperature was well below zero.

She walked along the street, straight ahead, with the soup-pan pressed against her stomach. It was burning her, but she paid no attention. Cold and heat crossed paths in her flesh. Curls of steam escaped from the rim of the lid, and vanished into the icy air, like her breath.

She walked right across the deserted town. Her footsteps barely crunched on the icy snow on the pavements. She was shaken by brief, jerky sobs; the soup split on her dress and her mascara ran down her cheeks. She moaned as she wept, and swallowed her tears, which were chapping her lips. Marek's name was howling silently in her mouth and throat, she was chewing on tears that tasted of slime.

When she reached the area around Divoká Sarka, she disappeared into the wood. She slipped while climbing up a bank, and as she fell she lost one of her ballet shoes, and half of the soup spilled on to the snow, along with the lid. She got back up and went on, still clutching her soup pan. Then she fell again, and this time she didn't get up. She was found two days later. Her soup pan was full of snow, her eyes were still open, and the flayed sole of her bare foot stuck out, like an imprint of her heart.

Prokop stroked the stone face; he was wiping away, ten years

121

late, his sister's tears. And for the first time the horror of death didn't make him feel pain in his flesh, or even his heart, but rather a torment of the soul and an acute feeling of responsibility for those who have died a cruel death. We are never done with the beings that it has been given to us to love, whatever form that love may take.

When Prokop finally stood up again, he noticed, a little further on, Olinka leaning with her back against the fresco of the Vision of Saint Hubert. Philip was holding her in his arms and they were kissing, just against the saint's knee.

5

For three nights in succession Prokop had a dream that was not actually a dream. He was completely baffled by this remarkable phenomenon, which was to haunt him ceaselessly from then on.

It happened while he was asleep, but it did not proceed, as normal dreams do, according to more or less coherent systems of images drawn from reality and memory. It didn't come to him in the form of images, but only through his flesh and skin. The experience was essentially surreal; it called on an absolute memory and its effects were both mental and physical. Nothing had prepared Prokop for this journey outside himself: nothing except perhaps more than half a century of existence, and the fact that over the years his inner world had been continually adrift.

While Prokop was asleep in his bed, he felt that he was out in the courtyard, flying just above the tops of the trees. Heavily, very slowly and in complete silence, he was hovering up there in the darkness of a cold September night, stretched out with his back to the sky, his face to the ground, and his arms flattened against the sides of his body. His eyes were open, and in the darkness he could make out the massive shapes of the bushes and rose trees and the leaves of the lilac and apple trees hidden away under the foliage of the beeches, ashes and birches. He spotted a cat slipping smoothly between clumps of fern. Everything was a uniform charcoal grey. The moon, in its last quarter, was misted over with dull slate-blue clouds, and gave only a feeble light. As he brushed against the tops of the tallest trees, the dampness of the leaves penetrated his skin, he could smell their strong, rather pungent smell, and the rough bark of their branches scraped against his face and hands.

Nothing else happened that night apart from this slow-moving flight among the trees beneath his window. When he woke up the next morning, he knew that it hadn't been a dream. He really had flown in the courtyard. He could still smell the smell and the damp of the leaves on him, and feel the rough caress of the bark. His skin and all his senses bore witness to the reality of what had happened. It was a silent testimony, emanating from his whole body and asserting its authority through a rigorous language of sensation. Prokop couldn't be in any doubt about the truth of something that was still physically tangible, even though he hadn't the slightest idea how it could have happened. And he didn't try to find an explanation that day either. Instead he kept his attention focused all the time on the sensations he was still feeling on the surface of his skin, so that he could keep them from disappearing for as long as possible. They had made such a strong physical impression that Prokop didn't think about anything else; he just tried his best to sound out his flesh and find out how deep they had gone. And when he went to bed that night, it didn't even occur to him that this marvel might happen again. It did, however.

While he was fast asleep – it might have been around the first moments of dawn – Prokop took off on another flight. Once more his body, stretched out in the same way as the night before, scraped against the treetops. But this time the physical sensation was far more intense, so much so that he felt as if the leaves and bark were penetrating his skin. He was swimming through the dark, the branches, the silent hum of the night.

The substance of the darkness mingled with his flesh, the texture of the silence interwove itself with his veins and muscles, the sap of the trees seeped through to his blood, his heart grazed itself on the branches. And he was filled with a feeling of anguish welling up from long ages past and from the ends of the earth. It was an infinitely greater anxiety than any he had known before; it went beyond his person and his destiny alone, far, far beyond him, and all around him. It took on planetary dimensions.

The wound of History's most grievous, tragic torment, original sin, swelled painfully inside him, casting a multitude of echoes into his stupefied mind. But it was not just for Adam's sin that he felt this terrible sense of affliction, but even more for those of Cain, Pontius Pilate and Judas, and not only them, for all crimes committed by people against people, man against man, brother against brother.

Prokop's flight was growing more and more ponderous, and worse still, he felt confined. By now he was almost at a standstill above the tall linden tree whose boughs partly covered the branches of a twisted old apple tree, under which there were bushy clumps of shrubs, wild grasses and nettles. The darkness was particularly dense beneath this tangle of branches.

Prokop sensed a presence beneath him. He would have liked to go down and explore the undergrowth, but it was not in his power to go down or up, since he had no control at all over his flight. Held by the mass of the sins of the millennia in a strange state of weightlessness which seemed to deny its own laws, he was floating above a point of gravitation whose pull was becoming ever stronger.

The wind too was blowing harder, and soon a fine icy rain began to fall. Prokop remained suspended in his cosmic solitude, right next to the leaves which were lashing his face and upper body.

He awoke late, feeling numb and exhausted. He ran his hand over his face, and found that it was sticky. Was that because he'd sweated during his bad dream or was it the rain that had fallen in the night? But he couldn't stop to think over what had happened to him; he was late and had to rush off to a meeting at the publishing house. Until the evening he was too busy working, keeping appointments and meeting other obligations to think much about the huge emotion he had experienced during the night. But once he was back at home he could no longer hold his inner turmoil in check. In the course of the two previous nights he had been flung out of his body and taken to the outer limits of the most awesome of mysteries, to the very edge of the great forgotten spaces on the fringes of consciousness. Thinking back to that out-of-himself world he trembled, as much with fear as with desire for knowledge. He had been brutally thrown into the middle of a theatrical production in which the familiar and the supernatural came together as one. The meaning of that extravagant performance was beyond him, as was the reason for it, but he sensed that by gradual stages it was carrying a fundamental drama over into the concrete, visible and tangible world. The drama of sinful and sinning humanity, in fact. And he was not sure whether the thought of another visit to that theatre of shadows filled him with hope or dread.

Who was *he* in this drama? Just one more wretched actor among billions of others. Neither greater nor lesser than Lear, his Fool, Edmund, Gonerill or Regan, for when measured by the yardstick of sin no-one is sublime. Aloïs had died, blinded by the violent shadow thrown by the sublime; so had Romana, broken by the lie that smoulders in its flank. Both too much in love with the absolute, they had believed that beauty and salvation resided in acting, in art, in human love. But real life was still being acted out, in a different place and in a different way. It was a drama with no beginning, no end, and no script. 'I offer up this nothing in the darkness.' After which all words are superfluous.

Prokop went to bed as late as possible, expecting nothing – expecting the impossible. He fell straight into a deep sleep. Towards the end of the night the same remarkable thing happened again. His suspended body went off once more and prowled around the tall linden tree. Some washing hung out to dry on a balcony flapped gently in the wind. Now that the courtyard was so saturated with darkness, he could make out the colours of things better: the dark red of the last roses of September at the corner of the church, the pale matt silver of the zinc roof, the dusky ochre of the walls of the houses and the garnet red of the roofs, the various shades of dark green of the leaves, the muted, pallid gleam of the birch trunks, the burgundy-brown of the fallen apples in the blackish grass. And he could see his own body from the inside; it was the colour of obsidian. On the other side of the courtyard shone the feeble glow of a hall lamp, a faint straw-coloured halo which sprinkled its dusty light on to a patch of wall and some trees.

But Prokop was not looking there, he was peering into the dense accumulation of shadow beneath the linden tree. He now sensed, he knew that someone was down there, sitting on his heels among the undergrowth. He could picture his body, made of mist and tears and rockdust and smeared brown with dried blood. Even more clearly he could imagine him staring fixedly out into the dark, piercing its thickness with eyes that could never look away or close or light up, for ever deprived of rest and brightness, destined to keep eternal vigil in utter solitude. The eyes of a man exiled for centuries past and millennia to come in the desert of love.

Prokop could not get down to the level where this age-old man was crouching, cut off in silent anguish; he couldn't get near him or even look directly down at him. And yet he could feel, so strongly that it was unbearable, the absolute desolation of this fallen actor right at the heart of the drama of humanity – and of God.

Which one was it? Cain, Pilate or perhaps Judas? The jealous, murdering brother, the traitor with his hands for ever frozen by the purifying water in which nothing shone but the blinding light of his own cowardice, or the traitor whose lips bled endlessly from the wound inflicted by a false-hearted kiss?

The distress of this man cut off from divine mercy rose up to Prokop and swept into his consciousness, silently demolishing the ramparts of neglectfulness, indifference and lack of concern that until then had surrounded it. He felt the same icy cold that the man felt, and his own flesh was inflamed with the festering wound of remorse which endlessly gnawed at the other's terror-stricken heart. He struggled and struggled to get closer to him, mustering all his strength and striving to cleave through the air and get down to the undergrowth. But his body would not move; it was tangled up in the branches, and all he could do was hang there, helpless, in the damp, muggy air. His immaterial body was caught in the darkness, while the other beneath him expiated for all time the horror of a sin that remained gaping and irreparable.

Prokop would at least have liked to give a shout, to ask him his name, to call out to this man whom even death had rejected, who had no place in which to suffer his eternal insomnia but the unexplored reaches of the consciousness of the living. But Prokop couldn't use his voice any more than he could move.

And yet this stranger, this vagrant wandering on the outskirts of men's memory — whether it be Cain, Pilate or Iscariot — was waiting only for a gesture, a look or a word to be delivered at last from the curse which he himself had inflicted on his soul. But what man on this earth had enough love within him to rescue this irredeemable outcast?

No-one had that power — but at the same time no-one had the right to turn away from his torment and disregard it.

The more Prokop endeavoured to reach down to this lowest of fallen beings, the more futile his struggle proved to be, and the more he felt rising up in him the only words that would do to describe the untouchable one: my brother.

> *Come on, my boy. How dost my boy? Art cold?*
> *I am cold myself.*

But the outcast knew nothing of his concern, and even if he had finally heard Prokop's call, he couldn't have reached out his face or his hand to receive the tender compassion of his brother in distress without first answering, as Lear did to Gloucester:

'Let me wipe it first; it smells of mortality.'

The face, hand, heart and mind of the unreachable man crouching down amid the undergrowth smelt all the more tragically of death because there was even more at stake than the blood of a man spilt by his brother. The afflicted soul of this outcast smelt of the sweat of the blood and tears of God.

Neither Judas nor Pontius Pilate was able to rid himself of this fetid stench of treason and cowardice; it clings to their souls for all eternity. If either of them were to stretch out a hand, it would reek of the most tragic mortality. They await the end of time. Occasionally they pass through the outer reaches of consciousness of living people, who are left for ever after gazing off toward the horizon of their memory, without being able to reach it or even see it clearly: powerless, but aware now that they themselves are not exempt from coward-ice and treachery, that they themselves could have carried out the act of betrayal that brought a curse on these two men – their brothers in sin and supplication.

Prokop's immaterial body, stranded up in the branches of the tall linden tree, was an obsidian mirror which, as it blazed hotter and hotter, grew ever more distorting; the suffering of the sinner reverberated in him like a raging fire.

When Prokop awoke in his bed, the mystery of the night shut itself away inside him again without delivering its secret. And although after that he waited, night after night, in the hope that his body would fly off again around the linden tree and the puzzle would finally be solved, it was no use; nothing more happened. Sometimes he stood for a long time leaning on the windowsill, staring as hard as he could at the leaves on the trees. He thought of Slavík and his dog. Dog would have sensed the presence of that man hidden under the linden-tree, he would have alerted his master, and he might perhaps have known who the man was. But Dog was dead, Slavík had dis-appeared, and the stranger who had haunted the courtyard for three nights had gone off to endure his age-old torment else-where. There was no smell in the courtyard except the insipid odour of empty space, and no sense at all that the darkness would offer him another chance to fly. Sheets, shirts and babies' blankets hung like humble white flags of surrender and renunciation from balconies suspended in the desert of the night. All around the courtyard the high, ochre walls of buildings, pierced by the black rectangles of windows, stood in silence, looking like flat tombstones propped in the upright position. Now and again one of these black slabs was lit up for a moment, a silhouetted figure appeared in the fleeting light and disappeared almost immediately, then once again the tomb was plunged into leaden darkness.

Sometimes Prokop had doubts about his completeness as a living being, about whether he was fully present in the world. He doubted even more whether the dead were really absent. There were times when he felt that he was a renegade wandering between one camp and the other, but never finding a place where he really belonged.

Winter came. The scenery of the drama which Prokop had witnessed three times – and even taken part in without in the least understanding the rôle he was playing – came down. There was not a leaf or blade of grass left swaying in the courtyard: only tree-trunks and bare branches. The ground was bare and blackened, and all the birdsong had gone except for the raucous cry of the rooks. At the foot of the tall, bare linden tree and the twisted apple tree, the frozen earth bore no traces.

The traces were drifting about somewhere deep in his mind. Every now and then Prokop took a wander round them, tiptoeing hesitantly. A confused fear held him back from venturing any further into those unlimited spaces which he had glimpsed beyond the bounds of his own consciousness. He had a strong feeling that if he was crazy enough to go any further, he would never find his way back. All he could do was survey the threshold.

6

One morning Prokop was woken early by the telephone ringing. It was a call from the psychiatric hospital where his

129

daughter had just been taken. It was nothing very serious, he
was told, just a fit of hysterics which admittedly could have
had dire consequences if action hadn't been taken in time.
Anyway, the worst was over, at least they assumed so. Prokop
had no idea what they were talking about, but since he tended
to think that when the worst happens, it inevitably means that
there is still worse to come, he rushed by taxi to the hospital,
where he was a given a cold reception and only allowed to see
Olinka very briefly. She was asleep, knocked out by the saving
grace of a sleep-inducing chemical. She looked very pale;
there were dressings on her hands and arms and scratches
on her face. Her hennaed hair stuck to her forehead and
temples, and she had large purple rings in the hollows
round her eyes. Prokop leant over his daughter and clumsily
tried to bring some order to her tangle of orangey hair.
Meanwhile he could do nothing at all to sort out the chaos
that was going on in his own mind. He looked around for
Philip, but was told that no young man had been there. It
was the neighbours who had called the hospital. Prokop
looked in Olinka's bag for the keys of her flat and went off
to Braník.

The studio was in chaos. Everything was upside down,
several panes of glass were broken, and worst of all the plants
were lying in shreds all over the place. There were leaves
everywhere; someone had cut them to pieces with a knife, and
even the cacti had been slashed to bits. Prokop was gazing
flabbergasted at this scene of disaster, wondering who the
bloody bastard was who could possibly be responsible, when
there was a tap on the open door and a plump, little old
woman from a neighbouring flat came in, wanting to know
what was happening. Shortly afterwards she was joined by
another neighbour, a buxom forty-year-old wearing a very
tight bright pink frilly dressing-gown. Prokop asked what had
happened.

'Well . . . it was the girl who did it,' said the stout woman.
'And she's certainly made a nice mess, I must say! She
wrecked everything, and my goodness did she yell her head
off at the same time!'

'Oh yes, poor little thing, she shouted all right!' said the old woman, clasping her hands.

'But why?' asked Prokop, who was feeling more and more baffled. 'Wasn't her boyfriend there?'

'Hardly,' cried the fat woman, 'seeing that he's dumped her! That's why she cracked up, poor kid. He told her in the nicest possible way that he didn't love her any more, that he fancied someone else, and then he cleared off. Usual old story, eh? Saving your presence, it's always the same with men. But your little girl didn't know the rules of the game, and she took it very badly.'

'Just look at her poor plants,' wailed the old woman, looking around in some distress, 'and she loved them so much! Every time she went away for a few days she got me to come in and water them. How could she have done it?'

The old woman was talking about Olinka as if she were dead.

'Huh,' concluded the plump woman, 'plants are just like blokes, you can always get more of them. She'll get over it, she's still very young, don't you worry.'

Prokop didn't know which of these two women he felt more like hitting. He regained his composure, thanked the neighbours and politely got rid of them, then swept up all the bits and pieces that were strewn over the floor, and put the books and the few other things that weren't broken back where they belonged. But on further reflection he thought better of it. Olinka mustn't come back to this place. When she came out of hospital she would live with him. So he began to put away her belongings into bags, some of which he took away. As soon as he was back home he telephoned the hospital; Olinka was still sleeping. Then he called Magda to let her know what had happened. She made no comment, just said that she was going to come to Prague to see her daughter, then hung up.

The next day Magda was in Prague. Prokop met her in Olinka's bedroom. He hadn't seen her for several years. She had hardly changed at all; she was still beautiful, but her features were set in a hardened, bitter expression.

Olinka had woken up. She was calm, but appeared to be completely worn out. More than that, she seemed overwhelmed with grief. When she was spoken to she turned her face away and wept silently. She kept crumpling the edge of the sheets with her bandaged fingers, and she never spoke except to ask for something to drink. She was thirsty the whole time. Prokop remembered what she had told him about plants being thirsty, that they suffered as much as human beings when their thirst was not quenched. He remembered the way she had told him that, the odd words she had sometimes chosen to explain what she meant, and the inflections of her voice. When she talked about the plants being thirsty it was really another thirst she was talking about: a longing for infinity, a dream of eternity which she must at that time, in a confused way, have felt coming to life and unfolding within her. Her thirst had just been poisoned.

As they parted in the hall, Magda announced to Prokop that she had decided to take Olinka back to the country with her as soon as she was strong enough to come out of hospital. It was out of the question for Olinka to go and live with him at the moment; what right did he have to look after the child at this time of affliction, when he had left her fifteen years ago with the same arrogant, thoughtless cruelty as Philip? He had put her through the same thing as Olinka was going through now, and just as brutally. She had not forgotten, or forgiven. True, she had rebuilt her life, but on a foundation of inner ruins.

Magda said all that without looking at him. She kept her face turned away and talked in a muffled, almost toneless voice. A very bright blue vein showed through on her temple. A few moments earlier Prokop had noticed the same vein on Olinka's temple, and also that her nostrils quivered just like her mother's. The pain and anger brought on by scorned love registered the same signs in the bodies of both mother and daughter: a cold blueness and a delicate quivering which were destined little by little to harden their beauty. Prokop also noted that Magda never said 'their' daughter when talking about Olinka, but always 'her' daughter or 'this child', as if by being unfaithful as a husband he had simultaneously – and permanently – surrendered his status and rights as a father. She left without saying goodbye.

Prokop walked home; he needed to. He had not breathed a word during Magda's monologue. He knew that he had nothing to say in his own defence. It was true that when he had deserted Magda he hadn't bothered to think much about the effect it would have on her. He was far too wrapped up in his new love at the time. No-one counted but Marie. Passion justified all and absolved everything. Magda's suffering was written off as just one of those things that couldn't be helped. The lovely smile of one woman made it so easy to forget the tears of the other. And then it was his turn. When Marie left him, he found out all about the long, drawn-out purgatory of having to put yourself through a period of mourning for a person who meanwhile is alive and well and enjoying new-found happiness only a stone's throw away. But his own misfortune could in no way mitigate the wrong Prokop had done to Magda in the past. No wrong can be declared past history while the suffering it has engendered still continues.

Prokop kept walking, and four women's first names walked along with him, intermingling, jostling and stumbling in his head. Magda, Marie, Romana, Olinka . . . He didn't want bitterness and disillusionment to spoil Olinka's beauty and sour her features; but far more than that, he was terrified that she might succumb to despair. She had inherited the blue-mauve, crocus-coloured ink of her blood from Magda, and it might end up writing into her flesh the same shrill message of hate as it had written into her mother's. But there are other more obscure, secret legacies that slip in obliquely, outside the straight mother-daughter line, from indirect mothers and sisters who unwittingly pour white ink into the bodies of some of their descendants. It was possible that the pitiful death of Romana had imprinted itself, like a faint murmur of invisible ink, in Olinka.

133

Prokop walked the streets until evening. On his way he stopped in several bars and downed a large number of vodkas. By the time it got dark he was tired out, but he couldn't go to bed. There was still something going round and round in his mind. He sat down at his table and began to write. He had to speak to his daughter, and through her to his former wife, and most of all to his sister. And perhaps to himself as well. He didn't know what he was going to say. He closed his eyes for a moment, and searched for a word with which to begin. The word 'path' emerged from the chaos of language and caught his attention. That was enough. Perhaps it was because at that moment a memory of Mary Magdalene lying beside a path came shivering into his mind. But Prokop was in no state to pinpoint precise memories; he just let words come up to the surface and murmur in a confused babble. And then, with the word path as his starting-point, he made up an impromptu story for Olinka.

7

There was once a little dirt path. It meandered over the plain, far away from the big cities. Along its sides there were over-grown banks, poplars and silver birches, and rocks. At one of its meanders it brushed up against a stone cross with a plinth that was all covered in moss. Then it went off and got lost somewhere in the plain, among the brambles and dust. Worn out by so much vast space it eventually faded away under the short grass and pebbles, in the same way as the dead fade away when earth's night invites them to the great mystery of disappearance.

For paths have a life, a history and a destiny, just as people do. And like people, they die one day.

Their history is linked to that of the people who first marked them out, and to all those who have travelled along them. And they have a heart, a beating heart that resonates with the footsteps of the walkers who tread on them. Death comes to them when everyone deserts them, when no-one cares for them any more. When the footsteps fall silent, so do their hearts.

And so paths have a soul as well, and a voice. A very thin little voice which sometimes comes out and starts to sing, at the furthermost edge of silence.

The voices of paths sing of the loves, sorrows and joys of all those who have travelled along them; for they keep them all in their memory.

Their memory is faithful, as deep as the centuries.

So it was that one day the little dirt path revealed its song to a young girl. The young girl's footsteps were so light and so soft that they awakened feelings even in the earth and loose stones on which they stepped.

The young girl's name was Lulla. She had golden hair and slightly tapering, almond-shaped hazel eyes.

Lulla was walking without knowing where she was going. A sudden, terrible sorrow had driven her from her home in the middle of the night.

Lulla loved, and was not loved in return. It was the first time that she had discovered that anguish of the heart whose calls receive no answering echo and whose tears go unconsoled.

She walked straight ahead; then in the dawn mist she lost her way. She didn't turn back, she just kept going.

It didn't much matter to her where her steps were taking her. For her the world was a desolate wasteland. She loved, and was not loved in return. She needed an endless amount of space and silence to try to quieten the long lament that was moaning inside her. She had to take her sorrow far away, as far away as possible. And so it was that one day she found herself on the little dirt path which no-one ever walked on any more.

When the little path felt the young girl's steps tread on it, its old heart of earth and dust started to tremble, and as the girl walked along, its sleeping memory began to come back to life. Its voice awoke from its long silence, and spun a fine web of murmurs among the grasses on the bank.

At first Lulla was still too absorbed in her sadness to hear anything. Then the path sang out in a fuller, more resonant voice. Lulla thought it was the wind that was making these deep, slow sounds. But there was no wind blowing.

The singing went along with Lulla. It vibrated under her feet, until gradually she began to forget about her sorrow and look around to see where a voice that was singing so beautifully could be coming from.

When the path felt that the young girl was starting to pay attention, it wound its voice all around her body, embraced her chest and neck and sang right next to her skin. And then the words that the voice was chanting slowly became clear to Lulla.

They were simple, poor, everyday words that the path had picked up over the years from the footsteps of all the men and women who had once walked on its soil. But the path, from its age-old beginnings, from deep in the earth it was made of, from high, high in the sky that stretched above it to infinity, from the heart of nights as well as days, had drawn forth a tone of the utmost solemnity and sweetness.

Listen, young girl, murmured the voice to Lulla, listen to the song of an old path of the plains. Lend your ear and reach out with your heart, for I am a path of noble memory. I shall sing very close to you and in the hollows of your ears, I shall sing within you, in your flesh and in your blood, I shall sing under your skin. Let me even slip into your breath.

Listen, young girl, you who walk without knowing where you are going, I shall tell you of the vastness of the plain and the deep sorrow of the trees and rocks which can never know its infinite reaches. For they must stand still, tied down for ever to the dark earth by their long roots or the terrible weight of their own bulk.

I shall tell you of the great torment of the trees whose roots are at once nourishing and deadly. The deeper they go and the more they multiply, the more sap they suck up to make the tree grow strong and tall. And also, the more

136

they bind and enslave the mighty tree. It is never allowed to take even the slightest step.

The tree senses the space stretching out all around it, and reaches out its branches as if to touch that space and invite the wind to take it away to the elsewhere that beckons from all sides. But the playful wind just ruffles its foliage, carries off some of its leaves and abandons them soon after.

The tree strives to grow taller and ever taller, lifting its branches up towards the sky where nomad clouds drift lightly and swiftly, birds wheel, light ripples and stars glitter. But the tree can never fly. And its branches sag, heavy with fatigue; never to be embraced or caressed, they clasp one another and join together in silence.

Listen, young girl whose heart is grieving, I shall tell you of the trees' distress. Like men and animals they know thirst, exhaustion, hunger and cold. Often they have to wait a long time before the rain comes and quenches their thirst, washes the sour dust off them, or soothes their burns. They cannot even go off and look for a spring. I have seen trees in mortal agony for lack of water when they were parched by drought, or at the other end of the year, when their bark was bitten and cracked by frost. I have seen trees wrestling with violent winds and lashing rainstorms. They writhed in wild disarray, they groaned, rebelled, resisted. The storm tore their leaves to shreds and broke their branches.

I have seen others brought down by lightning. They suddenly seemed to rear up out of the ground, as if wild with pain, then beat the air with their incandescent branches. But their futile, panic-stricken flappings only has-tened their fall. When they crashed, the flesh of their wood was all black and petrified. But they died with dignity.

And even when they are dead, the trees go on waiting. They await the return of the birds whose songs are so deeply imprinted in the fibres of their wood. All trees, whether they be upright and vigorous or lying flat and broken, await the return of the birds who bring in their song the beauty of the earth, the taste of the sky and the wind, the splendour of daylight and the echo of faraway places.

Listen, young girl, you whose heart is closed to the goodness of the world, I shall tell you the secret of the trees' great happiness, of their unbelievable joy which nothing can destroy, not even the long ordeal of thirst or the slow agony of death from cold or storm, fire or the axe.

The secret is simple. It flows in their sap, shines in the green of their leaves and trembles in their flesh, like the birdsong with which it blends. It is called patience: a gentle, woody secret.

Look closely, young girl, you who roam to flee from your sorrow, look at the patience of the trees. It is more than patience, it is humility. They consent to everything: to being forced to stay forever in one place, to being doomed to solitude. However far their branches reach out, they never touch anything, either the horizon that surrounds them, or the sky with its ever-changing variations of movement and colour, or the other trees that grow alongside them. Sometimes they brush against each other, only just, with the ends of their branches. But the pleasure of embrace, the forgetfulness of self against the body of another, are for ever denied them. They feed on light, rain and dew, and they have no voice with which to express their complaints, desires and dreams, other than that which the wind is prepared to lend them from time to time when it ruffles their leaves.

Everything comes to them from outside themselves, from an elsewhere into which they cannot venture. They possess nothing in their own right, except for their patience. Things happen to them, but they don't hold on to them. They who are held without hope of deliverance by the force of the earth, keep nothing for themselves. They let their flowers bud and blossom right under the open sky, and then the flowers wilt. They let their fruits ripen, and birds of passage come and peck at them. They share their long-secreted vegetable manna out to the winds, the bees, the birds and to every kind of creepy-crawly. And they offer a shelter to any creature looking for refuge. They even give their shade: their wide blue shadow trembling on the earth that keeps them prisoner.

They feel no rancour or bitterness. They breathe out their sorrows in delicate odours and fine whispers. They carry children with intrepid dreams up to the highest point they could ever imagine in the vegetable kingdom, then they cradle them in their arms and teach them to look at the earth with new eyes and a gentler heart. And to look at the sky with an infinite gaze and a crystal-clear soul.

Consider, young girl, the patience of the trees which must stand still and wait for everything to be given to them, so that afterwards they may shower what they have received on other creatures.

Look up again, young girl, with your eyes whose lids are aching with tears, learn again how to see, consider the patience of the trees who keep endless watch, all day and all night long, their branches held aloft like the arms of men in prayer.

Receive their patience, for they even give freely of that. Welcome their patience, for it is humility, gentleness and infinite generosity.

It is a pure love, whose roots are gnarled and buckled by suffering. It is a prayer.

Listen, young girl, you who weep for not being loved, I shall tell you how great is the solitude of the stone cross that stands over there. No-one cares for it, it is forgotten and neglected.

No-one decorates it with flowers or bows before it. No-one curses it either. For there was a time when passers-by knelt and signed themselves in front of it, and there were some too who swore and spat at the foot of its plinth.

Both prayers and blasphemies fell silent long ago. But I have not forgotten them. I know that every prayer that was addressed to God in front of the stone cross was heard and received. And every prayer, whether of praise or of lamentation, left behind a murmuring in the stone and a sighing breath in the torso of the cross, so that the grain of the granite grew to be like a man's skin. I also know that every time someone spat at it, it was wounded as if by a vile outrage, like the betrayal of a brother, the disowning of a son, or a father's curse. And then I saw the surface of the stone sweat drops of blood.

Listen, young girl, you who weep for loving and not being loved in return, I shall tell you of the endless battle that this cross has to fight. Wind, rain and frost have eroded its stone, lichen eats away at it, spittle has soiled it. But it remains upright, with its arms open and its torso exposed in utter nakedness. It has infinite endurance. And yet its vulnerability is extreme. It resists in silence, yields to no temptation.

There are so many temptations for those who are wounded in love. Pride comes to offer its haughty grandeur and cold insolence. Hatred, quivering with violence, anger and lust for vengeance, rushes in to present its gleaming weapons. Oblivion uses a thousand cunning, seductive tricks to try and impose its sickly, spineless nothingness. And despair prowls round and round and says no to everything, except to death posing as its superior, consolation. The cross does not waver.

Listen, young girl, I shall tell you how these temptations reach their peak and torment the cross on certain nights in spring. Then the sky hangs darker and heavier over the earth, and a shrill silence spreads across the plain. The cross is gripped by an infinite suffering; suddenly the stone feels the pain of a body being beaten and scourged, the horror of flesh being pierced with nails. It endures the terror of a heart abandoned and renounced by all, and the anguish of a soul in mortal agony. The temptations haunt it, circle round its wounds like flames, and hiss in its fear.

The stone groans, streams with a mixture of sweat and tears, and gradually turns white and ever whiter, until it is transparent. The cross turns to glass through which the

black of the night gleams with the brilliance of a thunderstorm. Then the light turns leaden; and now the stone is
nothing more than a concretion of ashes, salt and spittle. It
has said no to the temptations. It has gone to the utmost
limits of renunciation and consent.

It is at this moment that a woman, who seems to have come
from nowhere, rushes barefoot into the cold of the night
and the silence of the plain. She runs to the cross, takes it in
her arms and pulls it down from the plinth. Although she is
in great haste, she carries out every movement with preci-
sion. She sits down on the plinth, lays the cross on her knees
and sings as she cradles it. She wipes the tears and blood still
pouring out from the stone of the cross with her hands, and
washes the stone with her singing. Her song turns to a
shroud and the palms of her hands become a winding sheet
on which the heart of the cross leaves its live imprint.

The woman neither sees nor hears the temptations
which lie in wait for her in her turn. She is bent over this
soiled, lacerated body, cradling it like a new-born baby. Her
singing is lost in the night, her tears tinkle out into the void,
her palms gape open to the sky. The earth is engulfed in
darkness.

Listen, young girl, you who would like to die for not
being loved, listen to the purest and plainest of songs, the
one that this woman sings as she cradles the body of her son
who has been put to death. And know that she will cradle
him until the end of the world, sitting numb with cold and
pain at the mouth of Hell.

Listen to the last cry of that son who loved as no other
has loved, yet dies alone. And know that he will love until
the end of the world, without ever succumbing to the
charms of the temptations.

And know that he will love until the end of time, torn
asunder at the mouth of Hell.

Walk, young girl, walk to the very end of your sorrow,
and sing all along your way, sing softly to keep away the
pride and hatred growling close behind you. Sing without

turning round, so that you can ward off the despair that lies in ambush at your feet.

Walk with your sorrow cradled in your arms like a sick child heavy with fever. Go on like that to the limits of your strength. Don't stop until you reach that bare cross standing over there. Lay down the weight of your wounded love at the foot of that cross for a moment – and that moment will be eternity. Then come back singing, still the same song. The very same one that I am murmuring in your footsteps, the poor man's song that I keep singing and singing in the hollows of your ears.

Your sadness will not fall away all at once, the lost love that you lament will not be restored; but it will be transfigured and little by little will become easier to bear. It will take a long, long time yet, but the trees will help by showering on you their endless gift of patience, and the river, the stones, the bushes, the birds and the odours of the earth will all help you too, humbly but with great goodness. And I, an old path which loses itself in the vastness of the plain, I give you my song, and sustain your footsteps.

Prokop put down his pen. He had written the whole thing at one go, pouring out all his anxieties in a confused series of images and sounds, and now he suddenly ground to a halt. He had gone as far as words would take him; silence opened up like a cliff-drop right there on the page in front of him.

So what had he written? Nothing at all so far that was likely to make Olinka feel better and give her back the will to live. These few pages wouldn't be enough to ensure that she didn't give in to the temptation of despair. He needed to find yet more words, ones that were more apt and more powerful. But he couldn't, and he wasn't going to be able to. How could he possibly translate into human language the inexpressible song of the earth? How could he transcribe in black and white the indescribable silence of God? How was it possible, how could anyone dare?

Prokop's hands lay splayed open on the table, among the sheets of scribbled sentences which already made no sense.

Writing and talking couldn't give comfort, and never would, for things that were beyond expression, too elusive to be pinned down by the language of words or signs.

Then, for the first time since Marie had left him, Prokop wept. Holding his forehead in the palms of his hands, he hiccoughed into the silence of his wordless, sleepless night, and as his tears flowed on to the sheets of paper they blotched the ink he had used to write Olinka's story. The sentences dissolved into mottled grey clouds, and the song of the path began to drift away.

Through the open window came the fine, sweet fragrance of the linden tree in full bloom. Its delicate perfume accentuated the strong, sickly odour of the tears that clung stickily to Prokop's face and hands.

Over on the terrace of Kuks castle, pitiful Death was quivering imperceptibly like a great black horse which has just sensed the approach of a new horsewoman, and Saint Hubert was kneeling in the Bethlehem forest and bowing his head in shame towards a knee that was bruised by the all too fickle kisses of men. Down at the bottom of the Divoká Sarka wood, a little snow from a past winter oozed out of the mossy earth. Prokop no longer knew where in his thoughts to turn; his mind went into a panic and ran like a will-o'-the-wisp through the forests of his memory, bumping into memories and images which his anxiety for Olinka distorted and brought to life as baneful phantoms.

8

Olinka stayed with her mother for over a month. Prokop telephoned regularly to find how she was. Magda answered his questions as curtly as possible. Olinka did not want to talk, she said. He sent his daughter cards, short letters, books, magazines. But he never got any reply. Olinka didn't want to write; she didn't even feel like reading. But she was all right, she was all right, Magda repeated coldly. At least, she would be all right, it was going to take time before she found peace of mind again. At the age of twenty Olinka's life was already being conjugated in the future indefinite tense.

All Prokop's time and energy was taken up with work. He was working harder and harder and going out less and less. In addition to his main job he was taking on a fair number of freelance commissions and translations of English and German articles in order to make ends meet at the end of the month. His rent was continually increasing, and prices were rocketing everywhere.

The trees were in blossom and the courtyard rang once more with birdsong. Prokop was happy enough; even though the tale of the old path had ended in tears, there was still a little bit of it humming away quietly in his heart.

One evening Prokop heard a radio broadcast of the *St John Passion*. He was listening with half an ear while at the same time looking things up in his dictionaries for a translation that had to be done by the next day. It wasn't long, however, before Bach's music got the upper hand. He was not really following, but every time the choir broke in his attention was caught. During the recitative the singers articulated the words clearly and the instruments gently pointed up their voices. But when the choir began to sing, both the music and the voices swelled with such intensity of feeling and with such a rush of speed that the air seemed to pulsate.

Soon Prokop was getting the same pulsating feeling during the arias with chorale as well, even though the pace was less hectic. Then these flashing, sparkling echoes took over the entire room – everything around him, and his body: and then all at once, his soul as well.

Da capo. Over and over again the melodies repeated themselves from the beginning, in a tremendous interplay of distortion, resonance and turbulence, well after the concert was over. The great pulsating swell went on into the silence of the night, mingling with the warm odour of earth and leaves which was coming in through the window, and growing in Prokop's flesh until he felt elated and dizzy. 'Herr, unser Herrscher . . .'

The pulsing beats became so powerful that Prokop could gradually feel them breaking down the confines of his inner being. His body was opening up, he was digging deep within himself, and his spirit was gaping open like a chasm overflowing with darkness.

'Herr, unser Herrscher, dessen Ruhm in allen Landen herrlich ist! . . .'

But what were these footsteps that were walking in his heart and trampling on his consciousness?

They rang and echoed through him endlessly. Their pace was fast, their resonance cavernous and yet deafening.

Whose were these feet that were filling the night with their rhythmic pounding, and Prokop's flesh with immeasurable terror?

And now the steps were almost dancing.

They were dancing in Hell.

Da capo. Prokop could hardly breathe. 'Herr, unser Herrscher . . .' He was running out of breath from following the rhythm of these drummings that were shaking the night to the core: a night out of space and time, in which a whole people of fossilised souls was held in the terrifying grip of an eternal insomnia to which they had all, by their own free choice, condemned themselves, by refusing to respond to love on earth.

They were all beings who during their lives had said no – a great, arrogant, irrevocable no – to the Spirit. They had denied the Spirit and repudiated the mystery of love in the furthest reaches of their consciousness. They had laughed haughtily at the words pity, mercy and charity: shameful, nauseating words that were used only by little, weak, defeated people. They had smugly claimed the right to nothingness, and day after day had prepared for their entry into that great painless void. But when death came, it wasn't to the nothingness in whose name they had believed all was permitted that it took them – it was to the desert of love. There is no other Hell; and that desert resounds with the steps of Christ come down to seek the damned and rescue them from their suffering. But it is all in vain, because even Christ cannot undo the invisible chains which they alone have forged for themselves. Not even God can do it, precisely because of the absolute freedom that he has bestowed upon them. Christ walks round and round their desert, but he can never enter it. They hear the echo of his nomad love, they feel its incandescent breath quiver on the margins of their solitude, but they cannot let it come near. And their anguish is all the greater because they know at last that they are loved and love in return, but can never heal the breach.

Da capo. 'Herr, unser Herrscher . . .' Christ was running in a syncopated circular dance around the impenetrable desert of souls fossilised in their own self-disgust. 'Wohin? Wohin? . . .' The souls could hear his stamping feet hurrying to search for them alone, and wounding themselves on their silence. They were dancing compassion, forgiveness and the absolute of love: 'Wohin? Wohin? . . .' The fallen souls were too weighed down by self-loathing to rise up and follow them.

Prokop couldn't breathe except to the rhythm of the blows struck by the powerless Redeemer's feet, under which the world was sagging, rising up, and sagging again. The breath of all those souls who could not name love because they had once debased it, or ask for pity because they had always denied it, was flooding into his own breath in ever-growing waves. And he would have liked to give them his voice, to cry out for them, to say Lord, there they are, forgive them, comfort them at last!

Lord, there they are. Aber wohin? Wohin? No-one knows where the desert of love is.

Prokop would have liked to cry out, but he had lost his voice.

'Herr, unser Herrscher . . .' The Lord was running, he was pounding with his pierced feet against the breathless silence of Hell to make it yield. But the silence of Hell would not yield, it reverberated for all infinity with the haunting echo of the footsteps of mercy, and the dumb terror of souls which had assigned themselves to damnation.

The table was cluttered with files and dictionaries; Prokop thought with despair of the vanity of words. His mind was stripped bare of everything but the eternal suffering of the outcasts. 'Lord, have pity . . .' But the Lord who danced in Hell was bleeding with pity: a pity far more tragic than any he, simple-minded Prokop, could feel. Despite everything Prokop kept repeating his silent prayer. The man whose presence he had felt under the leaves of the tall linden tree last autumn had penetrated his soul. Whether he was Cain, Pilate or Iscariot or some other traitor to love did not matter. That man had become a throng and the throng was looking up from the depths of his soul into his consciousness with a gaze of unbearable pain.

Who would dare wish for salvation for himself alone when he has glimpsed, if only for a moment, the eyes of the fallen, gazing for ever in wild-eyed terror? Once that has happened, concern for those irredeemable, damned souls blots out all other thoughts. It may even blot out thought itself.

Everything died down into silence again. The leaves of the tall linden tree turned to stone in Prokop's heart, and its icy shadow began from that night on to grow thicker, slowly knitting itself into a solid mass. Although he did not yet know it, Prokop had just sent himself off into exile in the inexorable solitude of those who are deprived of God.

NOTHING

1

The flower had broken through. But as flowers go it was something of a disappointment. No sooner had it opened out than it started ripping its petals on the thorns that bristled all along its stem. It had barely come up to the light when already it was sagging and hanging down towards the ground. And the perfume it was giving off was not so much bitter as acrid.

At the first gust of wind, moreover, it shed its petals. Its bare heart lay on the soil and dried out.

But that didn't necessarily mean that its life was over. It was still on soil, so there was always a chance that it would flower again one day.

All Prokop knew was that his existence had veered off into yet another tense of the future. He now lived in the future absolute, right in the middle of a present that was often as dense, thick and stale as it could possibly be.

During the summer Olbram came to Prague. He had grown and changed so much that Prokop hardly recognised him. He looked like a bamboo shoot, and had the beginnings of a moustache and a falsetto voice. Worst of all he was bored. He dwelled on his boredom at great length and with morose delight. Games of ludo, naval battles and magic tricks had lost all their charm. He didn't even enjoy reading and drawing any more, or dream of becoming a seafaring adventurer or a conjurer. In fact he had run out of dreams altogether. His father, far from being so enchanted by the sight of him that his eyes took off into a soap bubble, bowed his head in discouragement.

Never mind, thought Prokop, let's wait until puberty has run its course, and then we'll see. No doubt he himself had been an annoying little twerp at that age too. He would just have liked to be able to look after his son more, to have him there near him for longer, but his relationship with him only lasted for a few weeks a year now, which didn't really give them enough time to get to know each other again. His son had been transplanted a little too far to the west, and more important, a little too early in his life, whereas he was still rooted a little too far to the east, and it was now getting rather late in his tired body and melancholy spirit.

As for Olinka, she had just gone through an altogether different period of change, from which she had emerged not just defiant, but distrustful and often bad-tempered. There again it would all be a matter of time, and above all of patience.

Not so with work, however, and money problems. They hardly ever seemed to let up, and Prokop was kept busy dealing with one crisis after another.

He had long since given up the luxury of daydreaming in the shade of his plaster flower. And in the meantime it had become so bumpy and cracked that it had eventually disintegrated, leaving nothing behind but a large grey stain.

One evening when he was in the toilet rummaging about in his toolbox in search of a screwdriver, Prokop was suddenly plunged into darkness. The fuses had just blown throughout the building. His first reaction was to stand stock-still with the box in his hands, turning his head to left and right as if the power failure was going to call out to him from some dark corner, peek-a-boo, here I am, come and get me.

Instead of pulling himself together, putting his tools down on the shelf and looking for a candle, Prokop sat down on the lid of the toilet with the box on his knees, and waited for the power cut to end. From time to time the wind, which was blowing in through the open skylight, made the little bell on the end of the toilet chain tinkle.

Prokop did not move. He kept his eyes open in the dark. He was not dreaming, or even thinking. He just sat there, with his hands lying still and lifeless among the tools. He could feel the cold metal of the hammer against his skin. He listened to the wind and the thin tinkling of the little bell. Then there was a burst of yelling from Mrs Slunecko. People came out on to their balconies and called out loudly to one another, as if the darkness had made them deaf. Prokop heard all this noise and bustle, but it didn't get through to him and he didn't react in any way. All he was listening to was the wind; and inside him there was a growing feeling of emptiness, mingled with the smooth cold of the hammer. From time to time the little bell rang tremulously in his head: in the great hollow space inside his cranium. Nothing was happening.

Nothing had ever happened. All those doubts that had tormented him so much, those anxieties, sometimes tragic, that had filled his spirit with terror and his heart with grief for the damned, suddenly seemed to him as meaningless and without foundation as the dazzling moments of joy and radiant tenderness which had uplifted his soul and made him think of God. Where was the love that for years had kept on springing to life in him, each time more fresh and strong, filling his whole being with wonder as often as with fear? All of a sudden it had gone, leaving nothing behind – far less even than his human loves and carnal passions. Nothing: plain, dull nothing. Not even a single ounce of emotion.

The faith that had come to him by such long and tortuous paths was falling away from his heart, without warning, like a dead skin. And it was not even leaving a scar behind, as lost loves do; it was forming a callus. The name God, the words grace, eternity, salvation and damnation, were reduced to the paltry dimensions of mere technical terms. There was no echo in them, no emotion. As far as he was concerned there was more reality in the core of words like dragon, unicorn, siren or philosopher's stone. At least they still had the power to make him dream. Prokop would gladly have said to himself, the joke's over, let's stop the whining and get back to serious business. But he wasn't even up to trotting out platitudes, or anything else for that matter. What's more, he would have found it very difficult to decide what the serious business was. He was just a hollow, empty vessel. It seemed as if the frenetic rush throughout the country to restore property to private ownership was spreading like gangrene to the realm of assets that were intangible and invisible. Gone were the days when you could rent all kinds of homes and offices at very reasonable prices. Now the owners were reclaiming their family inheritance and raising the bidding. So who had the splendour of God's name just been restored to? To some cynical, brilliant illusionist, no doubt. It wasn't just in the field of human relationships that love was turning out to be a very unreliable commodity, of such fluctuating market value that it could plummet overnight from peak price to rock-bottom; the same applied to spiritual matters too.

The light came on again. Prokop blinked and came out of his torpor. As he stood up he groaned; his back hurt. Not only was the whole thing a dead loss, not only was God a mere toy balloon which had just gone pop, but on top of that his blasted lumbago was coming back. He remembered what he had come to fetch from his toolbox – a screwdriver to go and bleed the radiators.

The days and weeks went by, on the surface of things, on the surface of time. Nothing surprising happened to Prokop any more. There were no jolts or visitations, no dreams by day or visions by night, or heady spells of doubt at the very brink of the mystery of God. The ebb and flow of grace had ceased, Prokop's heart was becalmed and his soul ossified in the absence of God – worse still, in his non-existence. The great empty vessel that was Prokop had a hollow ring and a stale, musty smell.

Even so he felt around inside himself now and again, to check whether he really was empty. He just couldn't reconcile himself to this absolute fall from grace that had come upon him for no apparent reason. But try as he might, he found nothing, except for a painless callus in the place where his soul should have been.

Strangers' faces, far from radiating haloes and opening up unsuspected horizons, were leaden. Faces and bodies were just corruptible matter, skin and fat, muscles and nerves. There were even days when the faces of people he saw in the street or in the underground or the tram changed shape and turned into grimacing masks with hideous noses which he found utterly repulsive. They were just ugly, bulging, misshapen snouts with no possible purpose other than sniffing at dust and filth. And at times like that he felt sick with pity for those around him and complete disgust for himself.

Some evenings he would stand at his window for a while and look out into the courtyard, peering into the shapeless, black mass of the foliage. He would stare for a long time at the linden tree until he could distinguish each leaf, shaped like a very smooth, veined heart. He kept hoping against hope that this myriad of silver-green hearts, lit up from time to time by the staircase windows, would give forth a sign, or a murmuring voice. Crazier still, he hoped that all the leaves would suddenly stand up straight like Dog's ears, and a trembling smile would appear in the branches. He stood there, leaning forward, searching through the vague recollections which were stored away inside him, trying to bring back to life the memory of the times when he used to fly just above this dense leafy mass. But all he could feel was the dismal weight of his own body. There was no hint of a presence under the leafy branches, no call coming up from the earth, no supplication rising out of the darkness. The tree was empty, the earth and the night were silent, the sky was horizontal and life was completely flat. Prokop was no longer in thrall to the splendour and terror of the Elsewhere. He was just a human animal, chewing the cud of emptiness as he trudged towards the twilight of his life. The emptiness was all the more bitter because he was walking alone. He had no-one beside him, and there was no chance now that anyone would come along and alleviate his solitude. At nearly sixty, Prokop no longer expected or hoped for a new love. Knowing that he was unloved, he felt completely unlovable, and spent more and more time going over the things he disliked about himself with a fine toothcomb. The self-love of the past had turned to bitter disillusionment. He felt cheated, by everyone and by himself, both in the world beyond and here on earth below. But this sense of grievance, of love betrayed, didn't even open up chasms in him any more, like the ones Romana and Aloïs had toppled into. There were no gulfs or volcanoes, just a flat silty expanse of boredom and world-weariness. No wonder that other people, when seen against a background like that, looked like mere puppet figures limping along pathetically in silhouette.

All day long he evaded his boredom by working, then at night he listened to the hum of silence and eventually fell asleep feeling sluggish and sick. There were some evenings when his solitude had such a sharp, acid flavour that he felt as if he was biting into death and chewing on nothingness.

2

One November afternoon Prokop went with Marketa to the Malvazinky cemetery where Aloïs was buried. The sky was milky white and the city down below trembled imperceptibly under the veil of mist floating just above the roofs. Old women, laden with pots of chrysanthemums and tin watering-cans, pitter-pattered about among the graves. Marketa strode along with her head held high and her hands in her pockets. There was something different about her appearance which intrigued Prokop but which he couldn't quite pin down. It might have been the way she was holding herself very upright, or the stiffness in her walk, or the slight nervous tic which made her keep twitching her set lips as if she were constantly about to start speaking.

There was no slab over Aloïs' grave; it was just a simple mound covered with spruce branches at the far end of which stood a birch cross. Marketa took out of her shoulder-bag three little candles moulded into red glass pots. She lit them and set them among the spruce branches. The wicks sputtered into slender, pale, flickering little flames. Marketa stood up very straight, thrust her hands back into her pockets, and gazed ahead of her with a vacant, icy stare which, rather than seeing anything, seemed to be scouring her thorny, tangled thoughts.

Then she turned round abruptly and walked away, and Prokop joined her. As she began to slow down he went in front of her. They walked along a narrow path among the graves, some of which were covered with such an abundance of grass, flowers, plants, fir cones and cut branches that they looked like miniature gardens.

Suddenly Marketa began to speak in a rapid, jerky undertone. It wasn't Prokop she was talking to, just his back. All she wanted was a reflecting wall that would send back an amplified echo. He didn't turn round or even slow down, but instead of heading towards the exit he wandered off in a different direction and wended his way here and there through the paths.

They meandered about like this for a long time among the rows of graves, he in front, she behind. They went several times right along the wall of the columbarium and around the Field of Scattered Ashes which was strewn with a few withered carnations and some branches of shrubs. Marketa continued her muffled monologue. She was talking about Aloïs, but also about the child they had never had, and her own childhood, and her mother, an emotional cripple who had never held her in her arms or kissed her, and a doll she had had which she had called by her mother's Christian name in order to maximise the enjoyment she got out of slapping and hitting it, and about the first love she had had when she was about sixteen, and the fact that she had wanted to emigrate but had never dared to go through with it. All of this came out in a muddle; she was walking and talking like a sleepwalker. Her words hammered on Prokop's back like showers of hailstones.

The light was fading, and a chalky fog hung over the city. But the light in the cemetery had a different quality from the dusty haze outside its walls. Prokop was always amazed by the different nuances of colour that light took on within the same city depending on the place that was reflecting it. It was not the same in a school playground as it was in the streets, or on station platforms, parks, gymnasiums or the banks of the river, because light doesn't just reflect off earth, stones, metal, water, roofs, window-panes and vegetation, but also off the faces, hands, eyelids and lips of people. And their gestures, footsteps and voices stir it up, sharpen and bend it. And perhaps, even more than that, there is a web, composed of the fleeting dreams of the living and the indecipherable dreams of the dead, which coats the atmosphere of a place with silver.

In the enclosed space of a cemetery that silver coating on the air is very distinctive. It comes from the mixture of absence and presence, memory and oblivion, sorrow, tenderness, silence, flickering little flames and greenery which forms and condenses there, and the strange alchemy of the flesh that seeps through to the trees and the grass, or flies away in ashes.

Who could tell whether it was the bark of the birch cross on Aloïs' grave, the gravel on the paths, the ashy grass of the Scattering Field or Marketa's lips that silvered the Malvazinky air and reflected the light that day?

All light is a wind which holds within it tiny grains of the endless night that went before it, out of whose depths it was born and from whose darkness it tore itself away. All light is a dialogue between the spirit and matter, a gentle brushing against the invisible. A mystery.

As she left the cemetery Marketa already seemed to have forgotten about her rambling reminiscences. The swell of memory brought on by the wind of light among the graves and birches of Malvazinky died down as the street turned blue in the twilight. Prokop walked Marketa back home then went down towards the underground station. One or two fragments of words left over from Marketa's monologue, some sparks of flame from the candles, a few birch shavings and a little light-dust whispered in his thoughts, which still had not recovered their normal weight and vigour. For the moment Prokop's spirit was just a dreary waste ground strewn with leftover ideas and tattered remnants of emotions. And he was not sure that his existence was any more substantial than the portraits of the dead that were displayed on the graves.

3

One evening in autumn Prokop was in Strahov, waiting for the number 22 tram. It was drizzling. There stood the statues of Ticho Brahé and Kepler, proudly sticking their necks out into the misty rain. Prokop shivered and hid his under the collar of his jacket. He crossed the street and started walking up and down the pavement. He passed the two astronomers frozen for all time in contemplation of the movements of the planets, and stopped in front of the Savoy hotel. The building was being demolished, and by now there was nothing left but the façade. Its windows gaped on to empty space, and rain-drops gleamed on the glass. For Prokop it was a place that brought back many memories of the past: of his time with Marie. He thought how long ago all that had been. He won-dered where the spirits of places went when their homes are ripped apart like this. Did they bed down in the earth under the new foundations, or did they take themselves off to wild, unspoiled places, far from the men who had destroyed the home they used to watch benevolently over? Perhaps the household god of the Savoy hotel had gone somewhere not far away, like the bottom of the castle moat, taking with him the tattered remnants of his memory – amongst which were the remnants of Marie's eyes, smile and body. The spirits of places were as elusive and ephemeral as human kisses: pallid will-o'-the-wisps that pirouette once or twice in the sun before vanishing into the mire.

Prokop walked back towards his stop. There was a noisy clanking noise. A 22 was arriving, but in the opposite direc-tion to Prokop's. Its dimly-lit, almost empty carriages trailed creakily along through the fog, then slowed down. At the far end of the second carriage a man was standing with his back leaning against the window. He was wearing a bronze-green corduroy cap and a dark grey heavy cotton jacket, and he was playing the saxophone. His head was rocking backwards and forwards, and at the same time his shoulders were swaying and rolling and his fingers were leaping about all over the keys of the instrument. As Prokop stood there on the pavement, looking through the tram window at the sax-playing passenger rolling his shoulders, he realised that it was Viktor. He hadn't seen him for nearly two years. Viktor didn't notice him; he was playing with his eyes shut.

The doors of the carriage opened. The music came belting out into the street, splashing the darkness with gold and vermilion sounds. For a moment or two Prokop was dazzled by this gleaming profusion of sound pouring forth from Viktor's swaying body. The notes bounced off the rails and the asphalt like a sudden hailstorm.

Viktor was blowing into his sax as if it were a horn of plenty. He was drawing his breath from the very depths of his belly and his soul, and throwing it straight out into the semi-darkness, like a drunken gold miner scattering out to the four winds great handfuls of the raw gold he has dug from the bowels of the earth. It was the jubilant song of the flesh, the shrill cry of a heart in pain, the clamour of an overflowing memory, all at the hectic tempo of a love reeling between joy and sorrow. It was the sumptuous turmoil of desire, simultaneously marvelling and grieving to find itself still so healthy and vigorous in the midst of a world which it will soon be obliged to leave.

The doors closed again, and the tram rattled unsteadily off towards the White Mountain. Viktor's silhouette, framed in the brightness of the window, disappeared round the bend. Prokop crossed the street again to go and wait at his stop. The rhythm of the sax was still pulsating around him, hanging like dancing commas on to the grainy surface of the fog. At last his tram appeared down the hill. Like Viktor's it was virtually empty inside, but unlike his it was painted on both sides with advertisements for Camel cigarettes, featuring a garish display of deep blue camels outlined against an orangey-yellow background. This time when the tram stopped there was nothing to be heard except the doors opening as usual with a sound like a wheezing old accordion. Prokop rushed straight to the far end of the carriage and stood facing the window. The floor shook under his feet, and the whole passenger area pitched violently from side to side. The driver was leading his caravan of blue camels too roughly for comfort. The sepulchral façade of the Savoy hotel toppled over in the darkness.

The grating noise of the wheels grew even louder as the tram turned into Keplerová Street. A birch grove loomed out of the darkness, was lit up for a moment, then plunged back into its ashy limbo. Prokop jolted and shook as the vehicle bumped and rattled. As he watched the line of trees along Jelení Avenue go by, he caught fleeting glimpses of the bunches of coral red berries among the leaves of the rowan-trees, the silvery shiver running through the poplars, and the soft green, half-open husks on the branches of the chestnut trees which occasionally lashed against the windows of the carriage.

With the night on his tail and a herd of camels being whipped by trees on either side of him, Prokop was conscious of nothing but the tram's relentless progress along the tracks. Inside him, waves of saxophone music slapped and foamed against his chest, spurting wildly into the void that had beset his spirit for so long. And in fits and starts his spirit came back to life.

Viktor, playing alone at the back of his tram, gave his music as an absolute and unconditional gift. He went all over the city and right out into the suburbs, offering his song to whoever wanted to hear it, to the people in the street, the statues and the stars. He gave everything, by giving of himself in an upsurge of the purest, most selfless generosity. He scattered into the darkness the song of the world – the true Story of how time passes, gives life and movement, and carries all away with it. And he was able to express that without uttering a word or quivering with silent tears of impotence. He spoke as a prophet sent by the earth alone, in the name of all beings of flesh and desire, with the mouth and breath of a living mortal.

If God existed, well and good, but then let Him hear this song of man glorifying the earth and exalting his love of the world here below from which he knows he will soon be cast out. Let God listen to this cry of man who, for his part, will never know whether God can hear him or not.

161

As the tram flew past the Belvedere garden, the waves inside Prokop changed direction and his thoughts did a sudden about-turn. All the questions which haunted him, which he considered so vitally important that every day his despair at not being able to answer them grew more burdensome and malignant, suddenly seemed pointless.

The tram was hurtling round the bends of Chotkova Road, down towards the city whose roofs and domes huddled close together in the mauve-grey mist like men's shoulders battling against the cold, against loneliness and fear of the dark. The hollow void which for so long had been digging deeper and deeper into Prokop came to a halt – but instead of filling up again with matter and light, it opened itself up to infinity. And suddenly Prokop consented to everything, without the slightest reserve: to being destitute of human love, and even more fundamentally deprived by the absence of God.

He was alone, with no guarantee of security at all either here on earth or over there in eternity. Well, so what? It was just the same for most of his fellow men, and there was really no reason to wail in despair about it, or even yawn with boredom. It wouldn't stop him going on living, and always showing a quiet, persistent concern for other people, both living and dead. If God was anywhere, perhaps it was in the shadow of every human being. But it didn't much matter if the shadow was empty and the horizon bare. It remained the case that everyone carried a shadow in his footsteps, and that the horizon rose up around the edges of every place. And there was life, with its longing for eternity embedded in every moment and in the very heart of the simplest things. That was enough; it would have to be enough. That was how Mr Slavík had been living for a long time: with nothing in the way of love except the wonderful memory of his dog's smile.

The tram was now plunging in under the arches of Letenská Street. Prokop knew nothing about anything. He had empty hands, a sadly neglected heart and a fallow future ahead. He gave free rein to the humble urge to consent to his own fall from grace.

162

Jolting along just beneath the Petřín orchards, the tram gradually filled up with more passengers. On the other side of the hill, Viktor was roaming off towards the suburbs, and an endless profusion of jubilant radiance was ringing out from his prophet's saxophone into the vastly resonant silence of God. The festive music rang out in counterpoint to the sound of Christ's pierced feet trampling on the musty, acrid tears of the damned, and called the living back to where they belonged – in this world, with all its beauty and pain.

It is not for the living to follow the Master of Light along the path of tears He treads; for He, and He alone, is also the Lord of darkness. Standing in a floodlight of pure incandescence, with bare feet and flayed heels, He weeps at the edge of the moat surrounding his own kingdom.

No living man has enough compassion and understanding of love to go down to Hell and trample the darkness with those tender, pleading, dancing footsteps. The feet of the living are far too heavy and enfettered to keep up with the rhythm of such a hectic, jarring, breathless incantation. To believe oneself capable of it is pure arrogance: an over-zealous, malign vanity. The feet of the living are restricted to walking on earth, amid the dust, stones and thorns, and stamping on the ground to keep their heads up in times of fatigue and discouragement. They cannot walk on water or on clouds or through flames, so how could they possibly dance in Hell? For the most part it is hard enough to walk straight ahead on earth, and even harder to keep going in the company of others. So who would dare claim they had the strength to go down to the depths of Hell and run endlessly around the fallen dead?

The living may well look towards this Hell sometimes, and believe that they can loiter for a moment on its borders and sense the terror of souls who have of their own volition exiled themselves as far as is possible from love. But they will never be able to enter it, or even really to understand what the tragic betrayal of love means. How could they when, during their time on earth, the sheer size and scope of the word love itself is beyond their comprehension. The best they can do is to receive into their hearts a concern for Cain, Pilate, Judas, and all the irredeemable sinners: to accept the collapse of the ramparts that encircle their conscious minds, let their thoughts gape open towards the wonders of the unknown, and allow the absolute of eternity to vibrate within them.

To receive, accept and consent, to listen to the silence and peer into the invisible: these are the noblest acts of care and consciousness that the living must accomplish. They must relinquish impatience, and give up longing for signs and feverishly searching for proofs. There are no signs except the impalpable ones, thinly scattered here and there, which sometimes, just for a fleeting moment, show through unexpectedly on the surface. They are unobtrusive but also disquieting. They give no certainty, but endlessly cause us to wonder, dream and wait.

As the tram crossed Legions Bridge, its reflected light trembled on the river, and for a moment reality and its double were one and the same. The real world had a multitude of doubles – shadows, reflections, echoes and resonances – hidden away in the recesses of its abundant flesh. Perhaps the imprint of God was concealed within it too, like a radiant hollow at the centre. It was just as likely that it had nothing inside it at all. Prokop didn't care any more. He had just, finally, given up everything, even the longing to be sure that God existed – even the torment that this uncertainty caused him.

He accepted the idea, the risk, that God might be an illusion among others, one of the craziest mirages among the multiplicity of dreams and desires that fringe the world and give it movement, expanse and breath. Even if that were true, it still seemed to him to be the most dazzling illusion of all. So why be alarmed, bitter or distressed in advance about the fact that the illusion might be destroyed on the day of death? Whatever happened Prokop would say at his last hour that he did not regret having given himself over to that wonderful illusion and let his thoughts wander at will in the splendour of that desert.

Infinity is so steadfastly present within our finite world, its waves swell up so strongly here, and the songs that come to us from its borders are so haunting and insistent, that we really must, somehow or other, make a little more room for it in ourselves and grant it some attention. It may even be that this infinity which groans under the weight of our indolence of spirit and meanness of heart, and howls in the cramped conditions of our finite world, is not just calling us towards itself, but inviting us to endless wanderings over in eternity, beyond the darkness. Whatever the case may be, there will come a day when infinity breaks its moorings within us and carries us away. It doesn't much matter where it will take us — to God or nothingness. All that counts is that one day, inevitably, the moorings are destined to be broken.

The tram raced into Národní Avenue. Prokop tacked through the hubbub of the city, through the glistening swirl of the real world, with the night at his stern and the unknown at his bow. He no longer knew anything, except that he was nothing. He offered himself up as such, in the darkness.

The tram bumped and jolted, screeching as it took corners and throwing the half-dozing passengers about. The drizzly rain dripped down the dirty windows. The smell of damp coats and parkas mingled with the stench of dust and rust which permeated the carriage. Even that stale, acrid smell of everyday life took Prokop by surprise and awoke his senses. He felt the commonplace nature of ordinary things so intensely that it filled him with wonder. Infinity trembled in the least of things, even in the mud that was spattered all over the floor of the carriage. Prokop felt himself the full brother of that crazy, fickle-hearted, stumbling child — humanity, his prodigal sister.

institut français

French Literature from Dedalus

French Language Literature in translation is an important part of Dedalus's list, with French being the language *par excellence* of literary fantasy.

Séraphita – Balzac 6.99
The Quest of the Absolute – Balzac 6.99
The Experience of the Night – Marcel Béalu 8.99
Episodes of Vathek – Beckford 6.99
The Devil in Love – Jacques Cazotte 5.99
Les Diaboliques – Barbey D'Aurevilly 7.99
Spirite (and Coffee Pot) – Theophile Gautier 6.99
Angels of Perversity – Remy de Gourmont 6.99
The Book of Nights – Sylvie Germain 8.99
Night of Amber – Sylvie Germain 8.99
Days of Anger – Sylvie Germain 8.99
The Medusa Child – Sylvie Germain 8.99
The Weeping Woman – Sylvie Germain 6.99
Infinite Possibilities – Sylvie Germain 8.99
Là-Bas – J. K. Huysmans 7.99
En Route – J. K. Huysmans 6.95
The Cathedral – J. K. Huysmans 7.99
The Oblate of St Benedict – J. K. Huysmans 7.99
Monsieur de Phocas – Jean Lorrain 8.99
Abbé Jules – Octave Mirbeau 8.99
Le Calvaire – Octave Mirbeau 7.99
The Diary of a Chambermaid – Octave Mirbeau 7.99
Torture Garden – Octave Mirbeau 7.99
Smarra & Trilby – Charles Nodier 6.99
Tales from the Saragossa Manuscript – Jan Potocki 5.99
Monsieur Venus – Rachilde 6.99

The Marquise de Sade – Rachilde 8.99
Enigma – Rezvani 8.99
The Mysteries of Paris – Eugene Sue 6.99
The Wandering Jew – Eugene Sue 9.99
Micromegas – Voltaire 4.95

Forthcoming titles include:

The Dedalus Book of French Horror – edited by Terry
Hale 9.99
L'Eclat du Sel – Sylvie Germain 8.99
L'Anglais décrit dans le château fermé – Pieyre de
Mandiargues 7.99

Anthologies featuring French Literature in translation:

The Dedalus Book of Decadence – ed Brian Stableford
7.99
The Second Dedalus Book of Decadence – ed Brian
Stableford 8.99
The Dedalus Book of Surrealism – ed Michael Richardson
8.99
Myth of the World: Surrealism 2 – ed Michael Richardson
8.99
The Dedalus Book of Medieval Literature – ed Brian
Murdoch 8.99
The Dedalus Book of Femmes Fatales – ed Brian
Stableford 7.99
The Dedalus Book of Sexual Ambiguity – ed Emma
Wilson 8.99
The Decadent Cookbook – Medlar Lucan & Durian Gray
8.99
The Decadent Gardener – Medlar Lucan & Durian Gray
8.99